A RING TO CLAIM
HIS LEGACY

RACHAEL THOMAS

MILLS & BOON

First Published in Great Britain 2018
by Mills & Boon, an imprint of HarperCollins*Publishers*
1 London Bridge Street, London, SE1 9GF

© 2018 Rachael Thomas

ISBN: 978-0-263-93496-0

MIX
Paper from
responsible sources
FSC C007454

This book is produced from independently certified FSC™ paper
to ensure responsible forest management.
For more information visit www.harpercollins.co.uk/green.

Printed and bound in Spain
by CPI, Barcelona

In October 2017 I trekked the Great Wall of China to raise funds for the British Heart Foundation, and this book is dedicated to my fellow trekkers: Tina & Colin, Wendy & Douglas, Glenn & Clair, Kathy, Daniela, Mary, Julia, Elaine, Martyne, Francesca, Lucy, Caroline, Rachel, Di, Brenda, Julia, Heather, Caroline, Chris, Jude, Taraa, Nikki, Richard, Daniel.

Also a massive thanks to Charity Challenge members Erika and Richard, and the amazing local guides Tony and Justin, and also Liz from the British Heart Foundation for making it such a great experience.

Thanks, everyone, for an amazing week and fantastic memories to last me a lifetime!

CHAPTER ONE

MARCO SILVIANO'S ATTENTION was completely capti-
vated by the curvy blonde woman who had just or-
dered champagne for herself and her friend. Even her
voice was incredibly sexy, and as for the bright blue
dress which shimmered in the subdued light of the
bar, intensifying his body's reaction to her every lus-
cious curve, it was nothing short of seductive.

He called the bartender over with a subtle move
of his hand. 'Tell the ladies the champagne is with
my compliments.'

'Yes, sir. Who shall I say?' the bartender asked.

He was here at this luxury island resort, his latest addition to the Silviano Leisure Group, to ensure
everything was being done exactly as he wanted it.
Experience had taught him it was best not to reveal
his true identity on arrival, but later, when he'd seen
everything first-hand, just as a guest would.

'Marco,' he said casually, not offering his surname.

He watched as the bartender passed on his message. The two women turned their attention from
the messenger and looked towards him, but it was
the gorgeous blonde who held his attention. Marco's
gaze locked with hers and something indescribable

arced across the distance between them. He took in a deep, sharp breath of shock. That had never happened before. He'd never experienced a sensation that everything or everyone else in the world had ceased to exist except for the person he was looking at.

He recovered himself quickly, reverting to his usual charm, and raised his glass to her. He was vaguely aware of her friend, raising her glass to him in thanks as she smiled and said something to the woman whose gaze was still locked with his. It was clear from the blonde's expression that she was as shocked as he was at what had just passed between them. The friend disappeared from his vision. All he could see was the blonde, her long, wavy hair cascading over her shoulders and resting on full breasts, tantalisingly concealed and yet alluringly revealed by her low-cut dress.

She smiled and raised her glass to him. It should have been an innocent gesture, but for some reason it was wildly erotic. Provocative. Heat surged to his groin and the promise his father and mother had all but forced out of him, to marry a nice girl and settle down, vanished like the setting sun.

He was here, masquerading as a guest for a week. The perfect excuse to escape the demands of a family he'd never really felt he belonged to. So much had happened recently, prompting the repeated question of when he was going to get married that he'd been driven from the New York headquarters of the Silviano Leisure Group, abandoning CEO decisions and board meetings just to escape his family's inquisition.

His father's recent heart attack had revealed huge family secrets, and all the times he'd tried and failed to live up to his father's expectations had come back to haunt him. Each memory had sat there around him, taunting him from the past. On top of that were the constant reminders that he alone was expected to provide the next Silviano heir—and his father was very keen that it be a boy.

His only sister, Bianca, had been dealt the unfair hand of not being able to have children, which now meant he was the *only* one who could provide the next Silviano heir to inherit all his grandfather had started when he'd emigrated from Italy to New York.

Maybe a little flirtation with this blonde would be just what he needed to distract himself. After all, he wasn't yet married, something he intended to avoid for as long as possible. His pulse leapt at the thought of indulging in some flirtation with this gorgeously curvy blonde. And why not? For one week he was far away from New York, far away from the pressures his family were putting on him. All too soon he would have to return to the reality of his life, but for now he had other far more important choices to make.

He slid off the bar stool and made his way towards the women and as he got closer the blonde's vivid blue eyes beckoned him flirtatiously, but the way she nervously bit at her lower lip almost knocked him off course. It was as if beneath the sexy flirting, she was not as used to the act as she wanted him to think. Could it be that the beauty of the island and being away from home was making her do things she wouldn't normally do too? Or was it the undeniable attraction which had slashed through the warm night air as their eyes had first met? Either way it

was an intoxicating cocktail. One he fully intended
to sample to the full.

'Thank you for the champagne,' her friend said as
she moved to stand behind the blonde woman, bla-
tantly trying to force him and her friend together.

'Yes, thank you.' The soft lilt of the blonde's voice
was not something he'd expected. The hint of hesitation in it didn't go with the bold and daring designer
dress which showcased her curves to perfection, making him want to hold her close, feel her against him,
then remove the blue silk and discover the pleasure
her sexy body promised.

'The pleasure is mine,' he said as he leant on the
bar, holding his glass of brandy, unable to do anything
else but look into those eyes. It was like diving into
the ocean and going down, deeper and deeper. He
could almost feel the water on his body. He blinked.
What was the matter with him? He'd spent too long
in recent weeks with his sister, who always talked
of him one day meeting *the right woman*, falling in
love, and despite her own heartache reminding him
of the son the family needed. Thankfully his father's
condition had meant that her constant remarks about
the expectation that he would marry and produce the
next Silviano heir had calmed as her attention became focused on their father. This he knew would
be short-lived.

The very notion of creating his own family was
completely alien to him. Marco lived life in the fast
lane, lived for the passion of a new affair. He didn't
want the comfort of family life when he'd failed mis-
erably to fit into his. As for love, which his sister
taunted him with, telling him one day it would get

him, that was definitely a no-go area. After discovering his mother's secret, the explanation as to why he'd never been able to gain his father's love, he wanted nothing to do with love—of any kind. He'd had very little as a child, believing he wasn't worthy of it. Now, as an adult, he had no intention of ever falling in love.

The blonde smiled up at him and heat surged through him as he anticipated the thrill of a new chase. 'This is Julie Masters and I'm Imogen...' She paused for a moment as if not wanting to divulge her true identity, her eyes searching his face. 'Just Imogen.'

First-name terms. That suited him perfectly. 'You look very beautiful tonight, *just* Imogen.' He smiled at her, aware his charm was having its usual effect and the anticipation of the outcome was more powerful than he'd experienced for a long time. 'I'm Marco.'

Imogen's eyelashes fluttered down briefly in a show of shyness that was at odds with the daring dress she wore, but when she looked back up her gaze was steady and firm.

'Hello, Marco.' Her voice had become breathy and very sexy, igniting the desire within him.

'And are you two lovely ladies enjoying the island?' he asked them both, in an attempt to cool the suddenly very hot atmosphere around them.

'It's absolutely amazing.' Enthusiasm sprang from Imogen's words. 'We only arrived last night, but already I am completely in love with the place.'

'It's divine.' Julie added her opinion then returned her attention to the champagne.

He couldn't hope for better feedback. Everything he'd seen since arriving this afternoon had pleased him, but to hear the island and his staff pleased his guests, the kind who could afford such luxurious surroundings, was far more satisfying. 'Where are you and Julie from?'

'London,' Julie said so quickly it startled him. 'Daddy told us to take some time away in the sunshine. So here we are.'

'You're sisters?' Marco looked from the blonde-haired Imogen to dark-haired Julie.

'Cousins,' Imogen said as Julie laughed as if at some secret joke and he doubted they were cousins. He had the impression he was becoming embroiled in some kind of personal joke, but, so long as that involved him and Imogen exploring the attraction which had sparked between them, he didn't care.

Imogen turned to Julie and a look passed between them, but he couldn't decipher if it was a warning, annoyance or shock. When Imogen looked back up at him, the smile was on her full lips and a sparkle of mischief was in her eyes. It notched up the heat of lust within him, made the sparks of attraction jump higher. 'And we are only here for a week.'

'Then we had better make the most of that week.' Marco watched as a flush of colour infused her cheeks and Imogen looked down into her glass, as if the bubbles could help her decide if she wanted to do exactly that.

'Just what I said.' Julie's laughter-filled voice snagged his attention from Imogen. 'So if you will excuse me, I'm going to go and do exactly that.'

Imogen's head lifted quickly and she looked briefly at him, before turning to look back at Julie. 'Is that so?'

'Yes.' Julie laughed as she was backing away, a skip almost in her step. 'Marco will keep you company, I'm sure.' Marco knew exactly what was going on. Julie had seen the spark of attraction between them and was playing at matchmaker.

He turned his attention back to Imogen. He liked her shyness. Surprisingly he found the idea of having to court a beautiful woman refreshing; instead of having them virtually fall at his feet—or into his bed. That was one of the things he now considered the downside of his wealth and family name. Women no longer saw him, they saw only what he could give them, but *just* Imogen seemed indifferent to all that, despite the designer dress she was wearing. He had the distinct impression such actions were much more the way of her cousin than her.

'I'm sorry about that,' Imogen said, shyness creeping back into her voice. This week was going to be a lot more interesting than he'd anticipated. The beautiful Imogen was just the antidote he needed before heading back to New York and facing the music. Maybe he'd even do the unthinkable and turn his phone off for a day or two, make his time here a moment of true escape. So long as it involved a night with Imogen he'd consider it worth doing. He wasn't about to turn his back on the high-voltage spark between them. He'd allow the attraction between them to develop naturally, something he'd never indulged in before. The thought of making the whole encounter longer, before the inevitable conclusion of hot, passionate sex, fired his desire even more. He was going to enjoy this chase.

'I have no objection to keeping you company,' he

said as she looked up at him and once again he was lost in the swirling blue of her eyes, only vaguely aware of Julie leaving. 'We have a bottle of champagne and the whole night ahead of us. What could be more perfect?'

Her coy smile made his breath catch and for once in his life, even if he hadn't decided to make it last, he wasn't at all sure what the outcome of this night would be. Underneath her flirtatious smiles and the enticingly sexy dress, he sensed Imogen might be different from any woman he'd ever had an affair with. He liked it. He liked the excitement which zipped through him because he would have to work for her, court her, in order to win her into his bed. It excited him because it was something he'd never had to do before.

'I'm not going to manage the entire bottle myself now that Julie has gone.' Imogen laughed softly, and again that coy smile. 'I'm not used to drinking it. The bubbles will go straight to my head.'

He frowned. Surely a society girl who was used to partying and being wined and dined was used to champagne. He dismissed the question from his mind, preferring the ever-increasing need to kiss this woman. 'Then I suggest we take our time.'

She looked at him from beneath lowered lashes as she tucked her hair behind her ear. It wasn't an attempt to flirt and not at all the usual kind of playing with hair that would leave him in no doubt the woman in question wanted him. It made her seem shy, wary of him. If she was really unused to male attention then he would have to abandon his usual seduction routine. A thought that filled him with anticipation.

'I'd like that,' she said with that lovely smile.

He put aside his brandy glass and with one nod at the bartender to bring the champagne on ice and fresh glasses he turned to Imogen. 'Shall we find somewhere more comfortable? A little more private perhaps?'

Briefly a look of panic rushed over Imogen's face, but then she shrugged her shoulders nonchalantly, her hair sliding off the bare skin, revealing the thin straps of the dress and far more of her creamy, soft breasts than he was sure she'd be happy with. It certainly stirred up the lust-filled passion in him, but it also made him question if she was in a relationship. He couldn't imagine why any sane man wouldn't want to keep this woman to himself, and he never became entangled with a woman if she was involved or married.

'Yes, that's a perfect idea.' Her voice was almost a whisper, which only added fuel to the fire of building desire within him.

He placed his hand in the small of her back, lightly pressing against her as they moved away from the bar to the more secluded areas surrounding the restaurant area.

'I hope that I am not treading on anyone's toes.' He pulled a seat out for her as the bartender brought the champagne bucket and glasses. Marco shook his head at him when he attempted to pour it.

Imogen frowned at him. 'Anyone's toes?'

He glanced at her left hand. No wedding ring. 'Surely a woman as beautiful as you must have a fiancé or boyfriend at home in London?'

Imogen blinked back the sharp stab of betrayal at the mention of a fiancé, but it wasn't this man's fault that

Gavin had walked out on her. The handsome and very charming Marco had no way of knowing Gavin had turned his back on her, on everything, just one week before she should have walked down the aisle with him. Or that Gavin had only recently married another woman after claiming marriage wasn't for him and that he'd only gone along with it because their families had pushed them into it.

'No boyfriend and no fiancé,' she said as lightly as she could, watching him expertly pour the champagne.

The light shone in his dark hair and his tanned complexion hinted at a Mediterranean heritage. He looked up at her and his inky black eyes met hers and she blushed, caught out in the act of appraising him.

He handed her a glass of champagne and she knew without doubt this was a man who moved in very different circles to the normal nine-to-five kind of life she led. Everything about him screamed wealth and power. He was completely out of her league. Imogen had no idea why she was doing this, why she'd gone along with Julie's suggestion and allowed herself to get so carried away with the fantasy of the island they had unexpectedly been sent to as part of their job.

She also had no idea why she, of all the women here tonight, was sitting at a romantic and very secluded table with the sexiest man in the bar. His tall, athletic body had stood out among all the other wealthy men in the restaurant as soon as she and Julie had arrived, but she'd kept her gaze averted. Men usually preferred Julie's tall, slender figure to her short and far curvier one. Inwardly she berated herself. Gavin might have knocked her confidence, but she wasn't going to allow him to send her back to the agony of bullying taunts from her schooldays.

She took the glass he offered her and knew this whole set-up was Julie's doing. It had been her idea to use their time on this luxurious island to escape their dreary lives. If their employer, Bespoke Luxury Travel, had seen fit to send them to Silviano Leisure Group's tropical island to sample the kind of luxury holidays the company could offer their clients, Julie had insisted they were going to live like those wealthy clients and sample everything—to the full.

Imogen just hadn't expected a man like Marco to be part of that plan. He was so different from any man she'd met, so very focused on what he wanted, which right now she was in no doubt was her. Acting the flirty and vivacious blonde wasn't her at all, but Julie's suggestion that she needed a wild, passionate affair to finally move on from Gavin's betrayal of last year had taken root in her mind. Imogen was once more happy and confident with her petite and curvy figure and wanted to prove as much to Julie.

No wonder Julie had practically pushed her at Marco. He was just the kind of man she'd label as a playboy: wealthy, handsome and lethally charming. Imogen smiled secretively to herself. She'd play the game, take up the challenge Julie had thrown her. This week she was going to be a very different Imogen than usual and make the most of tonight. Even if it was only for a few hours, she would live for this moment, as if nothing or no one else mattered. This was her moment and what better person to share it with than a man like Marco?

'I'm surprised a beautiful woman like you is alone

tonight, but I will admit to being happy about it.' Marco's deep, sexy voice pulled her well and truly back from her thoughts.

Just as it had the moment he'd come over to her, Imogen's heart skipped a beat and a host of butterflies took flight in her tummy. Her head was light already and she'd barely drunk any champagne. Could she really be an emotionally detached seductress? Could she really be all a man like Marco wanted?

'So am I.' She tried to remember all that Julie had said to her on the flight out. All the advice about forgetting *'that scum who left you virtually at the altar'* and living again. Julie had made her promise that the next time a man showed an interest in her she would forget the past and live only for the moment. No thoughts of the future and certainly no thoughts of the only other man she'd ever had a relationship with.

She smiled at the memory of how insistent Julie had been. She wouldn't be surprised if Julie was back in their luxury villa alone, just so she could force her to keep that promise and push her into Marco's arms. She'd show Julie—and herself—that she had moved on.

'You're smiling,' Marco said softly as he handed her a glass of potent bubbles.

'What's not to smile about? I'm in a beautiful place with very agreeable company.' She tried to tease, tried to flirt a little, but it was so out of her comfort zone. As was the silk dress which clung to each curve she usually tried to play down. The long front slit showed off her legs with each step and she tried hard to own it, to wear it. It was a dress which showcased her in a very different light. It was a dress for *just* Imogen.

'Very seductress,' Julie had said as she'd put on the shimmering gown of blue which had been part of the wardrobe provided for them both for the week to enable them to test the luxury resort and blend in. It was also something she could only dream of wearing and she hated to imagine how much it had cost.

'Only agreeable?' he teased as he sipped his champagne, his gaze holding hers, sending tingles of excitement down her spine.

She watched him drink, his handsome looks very Mediterranean, but his accent was unmistakably American. As he waited for her to answer, he lifted his dark brows suggestively, his eyes sparkling with sexy mischief.

'Okay,' she laughed. 'But it might inflate your ego too much. I'm in a beautiful place with a handsome man for company.'

'That's much better,' he laughed. 'So, *just* Imogen, what is it you do in London?'

Imogen nearly choked on the champagne as his question threw her off balance. Her thoughts raced as she scrabbled for something suitable to tell him. She was hardly going to tell a man like him, a man who emanated wealth from every pore of his sexy body, that she was merely an office worker living one monthly paycheque to the next. Why spoil the magic of the moment? Why not really live the dream and create a new life for herself?

'I'm a personal assistant.' She sipped her champagne then put the glass down, not wanting to drink too much too fast. 'What about you?'

'I'm in the leisure industry.'

'In America?'

He laughed. It was such a sexy laugh her stomach somersaulted and if she hadn't been sitting down she was sure she would have to because her knees would have weakened as desire began to slip over her body in a way she'd never known possible.

'That obvious?'

'A little, but you have Mediterranean looks.' What was she saying? She might as well have told him that she'd been studying him.

'My family originates from Sicily. My grandfather emigrated to New York with my grandmother when they were newlyweds to start a new life.' He smiled, and she guessed he must be or had been close to his grandparents. It seemed family was important to him, that he remembered his grandparents with the same fondness with which she remembered hers. Determined not to let her real life into this moment she pushed aside those thoughts and waited for him to continue. 'They opened a coffee shop and lived there all their lives.'

'That's so romantic.' The words slipped from her lips before she had time to think but judging by his expression it was not the way he would describe it. It also brought home that her first impression of him was right: this man was the type of man who didn't settle down, didn't commit to relationships, probably scorned romance and never used the word love.

'Are you a romantic?' His abrupt question backed up that thought.

She laughed and leaned forward to pick up her glass, aware of his eyes on her and the fact that her dress left more of her uncovered than it covered. It would have fitted Julie much better, her being so slim, but she'd insisted it was perfect on Imogen. She'd refused to even try it, reminding Imogen that she'd promised not to let Gavin's cruel taunts over her figure dent the confidence in her body she'd found after setting herself free from school-day bullying.

'Isn't everyone? A family story like that is kind of romantic.' She sat back and sipped her champagne, determined to keep her voice light. 'Do you not think it's romantic?'

'No.' The word was so final she almost felt sorry for him, but then she remembered where her romantic notions had got her—ditched during the final wedding-dress fitting. Maybe this Italian New Yorker had the right idea, maybe he didn't. Either way she was having fun teasing him. She hadn't felt so carefree for a long time.

'But look at this place. Romance is what it's all about.' She held her arms out and spread her palms upwards as she looked at the restaurant with candlelit tables for couples, the bar with its subdued lighting, the gardens they were now in, lit by lights which echoed the twinkling of the stars.

'Okay, I relent,' he laughed, melting her all over again.

'You do?' she teased further, laughing up at him as if she'd known him for years instead of barely hours.

He nodded in grudging agreement. 'Maybe this island is a little romantic.'

She laughed softly, aware of his gaze intensely on her. 'Now you are showing your Italian side.'

He moved a little closer to her. 'And do you like it?' This game of flirting was getting dangerous, but for some reason she didn't want it to stop. Maybe the champagne was making her bold.

'I do. Much better than your hard-edged-business-man-of-New-York side.'

'Ouch.' He picked up his glass and raised it to her. 'In that case I raise a toast to a romantic interlude on this island with a beautiful woman.'

Nobody had ever said she was beautiful before. At school taunts about her weight had followed her through each year, and as she'd turned into a teenager her mother had referred to it as puppy fat, meaning well but destroying any shred of confidence she'd had. Whatever the reason for her being plump and curvy, she'd never been able to look like her skinny cousins. Fed up with feeling sorry for herself, she'd decided to embrace what she had and, with a renewed confidence in herself, her lifelong friendship with Gavin had blossomed into romance. He was her first boyfriend and had become everything to her as she'd fallen in love. Yet even though they had been a couple for two years and had become engaged, he'd never once told her she was beautiful. As hard as she'd tried not to allow that to knock her confidence, it had, especially once their engagement had ended.

'To the romance of the moment,' she added to their toast, watching with a smile as his brows rose. Then without breaking eye contact he sipped his champagne. She could almost feel his body telling her he wanted her, could almost hear the words whispered on the warm evening breeze.

From the bar soft, seductive music drifted over to them, as if enticing them to make more of their moment. It was the perfect music for a slow dance with someone special. She listened and smiled sadly. She hadn't danced with a man for so long. Gavin had stopped taking her anywhere they would have to dance, barely taking her out on proper dates in the last year of their relationship. It should have been all the warning she needed to realise that he was just going along with their families' expectations, that he didn't really care for her, let alone love her. But she'd been blinded by her dreams of a happy-ever-after. She would never allow herself to be that fool-ish again.

'Would you care to dance?' Marco stood up and put out his hand to her. She looked up at him, his face partially in shadow because of their secluded location.

'But…' She stammered for words as all sorts of thoughts rushed through her mind. What would it feel like to take his hand, to be held by him, to press her-self against him? Heat surged through her, a warn-ing if nothing else that she was far from indifferent to this man.

'Shall we make the most of this romantic moment, this escape from reality?' He spoke as he took her hand in his, pulling her gently to her feet, then wait-ing for her to come towards him.

'How can I refuse?'

She moved in his direction and he stepped back away from their table and then turned to her, pull-ing her close to him. His eyes were heavy with de-sire and a spark of hot need that she'd never known before ignited within her.

'So,' he said softly as he looked down at her. '*Are* you here to escape, Imogen?'

'Aren't you?'

'In truth, yes, I am.' He held her even closer, his arms around her waist and his palms on her lower back, scorching through the elegant dress.

'Then we should escape together.' The words slipped far too easily from her lips and it had very little to do with the champagne. It had everything to do with the man she was moving slowly in time with to the distant music. Each move she made heightened her awareness of his strong, muscular physique beneath the stylish tuxedo. This moment wasn't romance. This moment was pure fiction. A dream she didn't want to wake from.

'My sentiments exactly.'

She stopped dancing and looked up at him. She'd never felt so dainty and fragile in her life. He was well over six feet tall, but it wasn't his height—it was the way he held her. The way he looked at her. He made her feel alive, sexy and desired. He made her feel beautiful.

Marco wasn't at first aware they had stopped dancing. He was so consumed by Imogen he could barely think straight. Holding her in his arms felt right. In some bizarre way she fitted like no other woman had ever done. Inwardly he swore. Playing along with this damn romance stuff was getting to him. He should just kiss her and take her to bed. Get her out of his system.

But he had all week. Time to savour this blonde beauty, time to be the kind of man he might have wanted to be if his mother hadn't kept from him one very important fact about his father. He pushed that aside. This was his time to escape and he intended to do exactly that. He would follow Imogen's example. One week out of his life, one week to be *just* Marco.

Imogen looked up at him with big blue eyes, so wide and innocent. Each deep breath she took made her breasts rise and fall, begging to be touched. If he held her really close she'd be in no doubt how much he desired her right now, but something was holding him back. He had no idea why, but, despite the heated lust he'd first felt as he'd seen her in the bar, he didn't want to kiss her—not yet anyway.

As thoughts of restraint rushed through the desire-clouded fog of his mind, Imogen moved in his arms, bringing her so close that she must know the effect she was having on him. A deep, throaty growl escaped him as she lowered her head, averting her face from him. He wanted nothing more than to lift her chin, make her look into his eyes and then cover her full lips with his. She looked up at him, as if knowing what he wanted, what he needed. The fight for restraint raged and by some miracle he only allowed himself to brush his lips lightly over hers.

It was enough. The touch tape of passion had been lit. Now it was only a question of how long the fuse would be before the inevitable explosion. Usually he craved instant gratification when he kissed a woman, not wanting to get caught up in the emotional warfare of anything remotely like courtship, but Imogen was different. This place was different. In a bid to escape his family, his reality, *he* was different.

If he was his usual self, he knew that once he kissed a woman passionately she would be in his bed that night. But not this time. For the first time he wanted to savour the moment, enjoy the mounting anticipation of kissing her properly, of caressing her sexy body, of finally making love to her.

He had one week here on the island, just as she did. What would it be like to make the moment last that long? What would it be like to romance her, court her—before the inevitable conclusion? Damn it. Imogen's talk of romance must have got to him.

'Are you busy tomorrow?' His voice cracked into a hoarse whisper as he moved back from her, away from the temptation to plunder her mouth. Right now she looked so kissable, so very sexy, it was almost more than he could bear. He had no idea where his restraint was coming from or what was driving it, but right now it was just what he needed.

'No.' Her whisper was husky and told him so much, told him she wanted him as much as he wanted her, that she too was fighting the tug of war between passion and restraint.

He smiled and brushed his lips lingeringly over hers. As desire erupted inside him like the roar of a lion he whispered against her lips, 'I'd like our moment of escape to go on for a little longer than just tonight.'

'I'd like that too.' He knew she was smiling. Her eyes sparkled as she looked into his and just when he thought he couldn't take it any more her eyes fluttered closed and her lips pressed against his. Soft and yielding, they tempted him, but he forced himself to return the light kiss, held on to his restraint as if his life depended on it as he avoided the kiss becoming demanding and hard. He wanted her in his bed, crying out as passion consumed them—but not tonight.

This moment out of time, this dalliance with the

kind of romantic ideas he'd always locked out of his life, had come at the perfect time. Everything else in his life was falling apart, threatening who he really was, and Imogen, a beautiful blonde, had slipped into his life. What better distraction than the woman who seemed as intent on escape as he was?

'I will bid you goodnight.' He pulled away from her, his body aching with unquenched desire. If he wanted this moment to last all week he had to walk away now. If he didn't let her go he wouldn't be truly escaping from everything he now knew he was.

CHAPTER TWO

IMOGEN HAD BEEN shocked by the way Marco had made her feel and even more astounded by the way she'd wanted to be kissed by him that first night. Now, after spending five blissful days in his company, escaping reality and living the dream of romance, what had shocked her more was that even though a sizzling chemistry surrounded them, he'd done nothing other than kiss her gently at the end of each day.

It was becoming too much and her whole body hummed with the kind of need only he could satisfy. Each day they'd explored the island and each night they'd acted like lovers but, when he did nothing more than kiss her, those old and supposedly buried insecurities had rushed back. Did he really like her? Desire her? There was definitely something between them, but whatever the attraction was it certainly wasn't enough for him to do more then gently kiss her and she was certain he wasn't the kind of man to hold out to gentlemanly instincts. He was a hot, sexy man and probably had women falling over themselves to be kissed by him—and much more.

'I see you have followed my instructions.' Marco's voice brought her up sharp as he arrived at the villa she and Julie were sharing, and when she looked at him that fizz of attraction she had each time she saw him rushed through her.

'As you weren't going to tell me where we are going or what we are doing other than it involves the sea, what else could I do?' She feigned indignation as she looked at him, feeling somewhat underdressed in her red one-piece and cover-up—the only two items of her own clothing she'd worn all week whilst she'd acted out the lifestyle of luxury.

'I'm impressed you aren't one of these women who cannot even think of going in the sea, much less getting her hair wet.' He took her hand and led her from the villa towards the beach. 'What is Julie doing for her last day? I hope she didn't mind me stealing you away again.'

If only he would steal her away for ever, Imogen thought, but she knew she wasn't his type. At least, the Imogen she really was certainly wasn't his type. Not that it really meant anything, she reminded herself sharply, the risk of getting carried away with it all stronger than ever. She was just someone for him to while away the week with. Why else would he have only kissed her goodnight at the end of each day?

'Julie is more than happy with our arrangement,' she said as they walked on the soft white sand of the beach, already heating up from the sun. Imogen wasn't about to enlighten Marco to the fact that Julie hadn't come back to the villa last night after her date. 'She's using this week to escape too.'

Imogen tried to make light of the whole situation, or arrangement as he'd openly called it. She simply wanted to enjoy this last day with Marco. Tomorrow she and Julie would be on a flight heading back to England and the normality of their day jobs at Bespoke Luxury Travel. Their moment of escape here on the romantic tropical island would be over.

'In that case we have all day to be together—apart from a little something extra I have arranged just for you. For our last night together.'

She looked up at him, the sun sparkling in his eyes. Or was that mischief? He'd arranged something for her? First he'd told her she was beautiful and now this. If she wasn't careful she'd lose all sense of reality and start wishing for the kind of happy-ever-afters she knew didn't really exist.

'I'm intrigued,' she teased but her breath caught as he took hold of her hand, making her stop, so that she could only stand and look up at him.

'I'm the one who is intrigued. By you.' His eyes darkened until they were completely black and her pulse raced as with his free hand he pushed back stray strands of her hair which had escaped from her ponytail.

He was going to kiss her—and she wanted him to. Not the soft, gentle kisses he'd given her since that first night. She wanted him to *really* kiss her.

Her eyes closed as he moved nearer, his hand sliding round to hold the back of her head, bringing her closer to him. Not that she needed any persuading. This was the last day of living the life of luxury. After tomorrow Marco would be part of a moment out of reality, a man she would never meet again. They lived in two completely different worlds.

His lips moved over hers and she kissed him back, demanding so much more from him. Fire leapt to life inside her as she pressed herself recklessly against him, abandoning any notion of being sensible, wanting only to ease her aching desire for this man.

He answered her demands with an almost burning passion as he deepened the kiss, holding her so tight. She could hardly breathe but she didn't want it to stop, didn't want the deep pulse of desire inside her to fade away to nothing. She wanted everything, every part of this man.

Between her thighs heat scorched. The hardness of his erection pressed against her made her ever more reckless as she moved her hips, wanting to get even closer, even more intimate. Her body was begging him to make love to her. She'd never experienced anything so powerful. Her ex-fiancé, her only other lover, had never aroused her like this, never made her so wanton, so consumed with desire.

'Have you any idea what you do to me?' Marco asked, each word a hoarse, passion-filled whisper.

'I do now,' she teased. Who was this woman? Imogen Fraser would never be as seductive and flirty as this. But she wasn't Imogen Fraser. She was *just* Imogen and this was her moment. Tomorrow it would end and she had no intention of going home with any *what if*s lingering in her mind.

He let her go and moved back a step, running one hand through his hair in a distracted way, which only made her want him more. 'Imogen—you will be the undoing of me.'

'I intend to be exactly that,' she said as she moved towards him, sliding her hands around his neck again and brushing her lips teasingly over his. The feral growl he tried hard to suppress left her in no doubt as to the effect she had on him. He did want her. He wanted her as much as she wanted him.

'Do you, now?' He put his arms back round her waist and she wished she'd had the courage to wear a bikini. She wanted to feel his hands on her body. Skin on skin.

'But first,' she mercilessly teased him, a big smile on her lips, 'haven't you arranged something for us?'

'I have.' Marco snatched at the change of subject she unwittingly offered because if he didn't he was in danger of taking her back to his villa and spending the day exploring the desire between them, which had now reached near explosive heights. Whilst it was very much what he wanted to do, it wasn't part of his plan to create the ultimate romantic escape on their last night. The pleasure her body promised would have to wait. 'We are going out on that yacht.'

She turned swiftly and looked to where a sleek white yacht was anchored in the bay, waiting patiently on the sparkling blue water. 'Now I understand the need for swimwear.' Her laughter was as infectious as it was captivating.

'We aren't just going on the sea—we are going under it. I've arranged for us to snorkel over one of the island's reefs.'

He braced himself for excuses. Any other woman he'd dated in recent years probably wouldn't paddle in the sea, let alone swim in it. All they'd wanted to do was sunbathe. Tiny bikinis were not for getting wet. Imogen's red one-piece showcased her sexy curves in a way a bikini couldn't, making him imagine how it would feel to have her naked body in his bed. Each time he looked at her, taking in every shapely curve, he grew more impatient for the conclusion to this week.

A spike of lust shot through him. He'd never waited this long to have sex with a woman. Imogen was different and, although he had no intention of trying to figure out why, he had every intention of bringing their romantic week, their escape from reality, to the conclusion he'd wanted from the very first moment he'd set eyes on her in that alluring blue dress. Tonight, no matter what, she would be his and the passion and desire he'd held in check all week could finally be set free.

'Marco, that's so exciting—thanks.' Her eyes sparkled like the sea beyond her as she looked up at him, then as if the wind had changed direction she lowered her head and looked down. 'Nobody has spoilt me like this before.'

A woman like Imogen must have had many admirers, all trying to impress her and win her affection. Her admission shocked him. 'I find that very hard to believe.'

She looked back up at him. 'It's true. I've only ever had one relationship. It lasted for over two years, but...' Her words trailed away, reminding him of the aura of innocence she sometimes portrayed. Had this teasing temptress really only had one lover?

'Whoever he was, he was a damn fool to let you go.' The words sprang from him before he had time to think and they were totally out of character. He never gave away his feelings, never said anything to a woman that could be misread as something more. Settling down had never been part of his big plan for life and yet here he was, talking with Imogen as if they shared a secret need to do just that.

'He didn't let me go,' she said, looking up at him, that spark of defiance in her eyes once more. 'He lost me.'

'Then his loss is my gain. And being here has enabled me to find you,' he said softly, brushing her cheek with the backs of his fingers.

'Yes, our week here has been fun, a real escape, and all I want is to make the most of the last day together.'

A sense of calm slipped over him. She was as good as telling him that once they left the island she wouldn't be looking for anything else from him. It was everything he had hoped for when he knew he would go home and inevitably throw himself into his work, the same as he always did. Anything to avoid the pleading of his mother to marry and continue the Silviano family name for his father. But this time he knew her secret. He knew the man lying in hospital with a serious heart condition, the man he'd never been able to please, wasn't his real father. Knowing that and knowing just who his real father was should have made everything easier, but it didn't. It made things harder than ever.

'That is exactly what I want,' he said as he forced his mind back to the present, back to the seduction of Imogen. It would be his last fling. He held her tighter and kissed her lightly once more. 'What I want is to enjoy our last day together. Our final night.'

Imogen slipped from the yacht into the crystal-clear waters, trying to push aside Marco's honesty. He didn't want anything more after they returned home. He didn't want to see her again, which was probably just as well, because once he knew she was just an ordinary girl, instead of the wealthy daddy's girl she'd let him believe she was, he wouldn't want anything to do with her and she couldn't stand the rejection of that. She'd had enough rejection recently.

Marco tapped her arm, pointing to a group of brightly coloured fish as they swam over the coral, and she refused to wallow in self-pity. She would take from this moment with Marco as much as she could—and she wanted everything. The passion, the desire. All of it. A shimmer of anticipation washed over her as she recalled his words on the beach: *'Our final night.'*

He wanted to be with her tonight and for one night she wanted nothing more than to be with Marco. Not the hard businessman she'd caught glimpses of all week, but the kind and caring man who'd been so respectful to her, not forcing her to do anything. It had been like the romance of an affair—but now she wanted the passion that went with it. She wanted Marco.

When they returned to the yacht she was deter-mined that she would have the entire dream of being here on the island with Marco. By tomorrow evening the real Imogen Fraser would be back and the care-free woman she'd been this week would be nothing more than a figment of her imagination. A memory to treasure.

'That was a wonderful experience,' she said as she ran her fingers through her hair, trying to tame the wet tangle. As she stood on the deck in the sunshine she was aware of Marco watching her, aware of his gaze on her body and all too aware of how her wet one-piece highlighted every curve. She didn't feel self-conscious, not when he looked at her like that, making her body ache for his touch, his caress. Right at this moment she felt alive. Sexy and full of confidence.

'You are a very sexy woman.' From where he was sitting, he reached out and held her thighs, pulling her towards him. Emboldened by the way he made her feel, she stood between his legs as he sat.

She looked down at him, his face still wet from the water as he looked up at her, and that connection sparked to life, dragging her deep under his spell. Did he really think that? She tested him, deploying her new-found confidence. 'Thin girls are sexy. It's the slim girls that men go for.'

'Oh, you've got that all wrong,' he said as he caressed her thigh, her skin drying instantly from the contact. 'Do you have any idea what you do to me?'

She shook her head, the shyness she'd been trying to hide surfacing once more, almost stopping her from having the one thing she wanted. This moment with Marco.

'Then I am going to have to make sure you know.' He moved her in closer, so close that if he wasn't looking up at her he could kiss her breasts. The thought made them tingle with anticipation. The heady pulse of desire started once more, deep inside her. His hands skimmed up either side of her waist, almost touching her breasts, and the real Imogen threatened to return, almost forcing her out of his embrace.

'I... I...' she stammered, the boldness she'd been

hiding behind all week suddenly vanishing as if the sea had washed it all away.

'Tonight is our last night and I want to spend it with you.' His hands slid back down the sides of her waist and her knees began to weaken as he smiled up at her. Damn him, he knew exactly what he was doing to her. 'Every minute of it.'

Her heart leapt. Every minute. He wanted to be with her all night. 'I want that too,' she whispered as his hands caressed her waist sensually, and she longed for him to touch her breasts, to finally light the fire which sparked and fizzed inside her, threatening to explode like a wayward firework.

'But I want tonight to be like no other, so I have arranged for something special.' He smiled, pulling her closer still.

'More special than this?' She could hardly whisper, her heart was thumping so hard.

'Yes.'

'And what is the dress code for this surprise?' Thankfully she found *just* Imogen's flirty nature, banishing Imogen Fraser from saying or doing anything. She fully intended to remain *just* Imogen a little while longer and have her night with Marco.

'Dress for dinner.'

'In that case—' Imogen pulled away from him, not trusting herself to stay in his embrace any longer, the heady need for him becoming stronger all the time '—I should get back. Have you any idea how long it takes to tame hair like mine?'

He laughed. A deep, sexy laugh which sent a shimmer of stars hurtling around her. 'I get the message.'

'Good, because if you want me to look the part then I will have to get back to the villa.'

'You already look the part as far as I am concerned, Imogen.' Seriousness had slipped back into his voice and desire in his eyes. 'Turn up exactly as you are and I will be happy.'

'You.' She pushed him away. 'Be careful what you wish for, Marco.'

CHAPTER THREE

MARCO'S BREATH WAS snatched away as Imogen opened the villa door to him. Gone was the sexy water nymph of this afternoon, with wet hair clinging to the sides of her face and that so very sexy red one-piece. In her place was the seductress who'd first captured his attention at the bar ordering champagne.

The kick of lust in his groin only added to the anticipation of what this evening would bring. Tonight, she would be his. For one more night he would live in the moment of total escape and forget the reality which would all too soon intrude, if his sister's latest text messages about his father were anything to go by. He pushed the thought aside. Now was not the time for those thoughts. Now was the time to lose himself, one last time, with Imogen.

'You look stunning.' Already his voice was hoarse with desire, but, from the look in her vibrant blue eyes, it was no different to how she was feeling.

She smiled and coyly pulled her hair forward over her shoulder, bare apart from the thin strap of the black dress which looked like ink and moulded to every curve he was impatient to explore. Tonight they would be in his private part of the island, and once the meal had been served they would be totally alone, and his plans to give Imogen a night to surpass any other she'd had with a man before could begin.

'And you look very handsome. A tuxedo suits you.' Even though she gave him a shy look, the anticipation of what was to come hung around her like the stars in the night sky. She sparkled and he knew without doubt that she felt the power of the attraction too. Imogen was as aware of the explosive tension between them as he was, and their conversation on the beach was enough to tell him she wanted this moment of escape to be special. Just as he did. A moment in which to lose themselves completely. A time to savour what they'd found before returning to reality.

He took her hand, lifting her fingers to his lips, kissing the tips of them. Her nails were a deep red and her skin delicately scented. He'd never known this anticipation, this sense of belonging before. 'Only the best for tonight,' he whispered softly as he looked into her eyes.

Her deep drawn-in breath gave away far more than he was sure she wanted to. 'More of your special arrangements?' she jested with him, that playful, teasing light in her eyes. 'You seem to have a lot of influence on the island.'

He wasn't about to tell her that he owned the entire island, not when she'd spent the week being with him simply because it was what they'd both wanted. He knew very little about her, but he did know that she wasn't at all like the kind of spoilt societal ladies he usually encountered as billionaire Marco Silviano. She seemed so in awe, so in wonder of everything his island offered, as if she was unused to such luxury.

But Julie's words about 'Daddy suggesting they take a luxury break' warned him she must be accustomed to such a world. Neither of them had talked much about their real lives and maybe that was for the best. She would linger in his memory, the perfect antidote to the constant friction between him and his family.

'I guess I do.' He smiled at her. 'And to prove it I have arranged for somewhere special for us on our last night. It's just a short ride in the utility vehicle.'

'Now I am intrigued.' She laughed and the way she reached out, placing her hand on his arm, sent a frenzy of fiery need hurtling through him, so fast he was in serious doubt if he could get through the meal he had planned without giving in to his desire for her.

'Then let us go,' he said as he held out his hand to help her in, trying not to think too much about where his thoughts had just led him. All he wanted was to enjoy the escape of tonight and be nothing more than Marco enjoying Imogen's company. Who they really were, what their lives really entailed, didn't matter one bit.

Imogen settled herself next to him and looked around her with interest as he manoeuvred the small buggy down the track which led to his private part of the island. He'd liked the place so much that during renovations he'd sectioned part of it off for his exclusive use. His own private retreat from his family and the constant pressure to be what he didn't want to be.

'And how many other ladies have you bestowed this kind of special treatment on?' There was laughter in her voice, but the nervous glance she cast him made him question if she wasn't as experienced as she'd had him believe all week. Like the moon slipping out from behind a cloud, innocence shone from her briefly, before being cloaked once more in the cloud of the seductress.

'None.' He stopped the vehicle at the top of his private beach where a table, set for two, was waiting. 'Now, if you have finished quizzing me, here is our table for us to enjoy dinner as the sun sets.'

'It's beautiful,' Imogen whispered as she stood beside him looking at the trail of lanterns lighting the way to the intimate table.

The sun was beginning to slip towards the horizon as he took her hand. 'I want this night to be special. A final night of escape with a beautiful woman in beautiful surroundings.'

'This truly is a night of escape, Marco. You have no idea how different this is from real life for me.'

Marco ignored the slight opening of the door to the real Imogen, not wanting anything to intrude. He took her hand and led her to the table, pulled out her chair and waited for her to sit down. As she sat on the chair, the temptation to kiss the soft skin of her neck, exposed because of the sexy way she'd piled her hair up, was too much. He leant down and traced a trail on her skin and a jolt of satisfaction shot through him as she trembled slightly.

The need to know more about this enigma of a woman got the better of him. 'Tell me about the real Imogen.'

She turned and looked up at him, her blue eyes wide. 'Not tonight,' she whispered seductively. 'Tonight I want to escape from everything. Tonight I want to be *just* Imogen and I want to be with you—all night.'

She might not be prepared to tell him about herself, but she had given him a loud and clear signal that she wanted him, that being with him was already a foregone conclusion. His pulse leapt with anticipation. After a week of nothing more than gentle kisses he knew he wouldn't have much restraint left, but he'd see this meal through, and then it would be time to put into motion the final part of his seduction plan.

Imogen had skilfully avoided talking about herself or her normal life all evening and now, as the stars were shining and the moon rising, she knew the moment she'd wanted since that very first kiss, when he'd bought her champagne, was finally here. All week she'd longed for more than the soft, lingering kisses he'd given her at the end of each night. She'd longed for him in a way she'd never experienced before, not even with the man she should have married.

'I have one more surprise,' Marco said, his voice husky as he walked across the beach holding her hand, the soft sound of the waves as seductive as being with Marco. She really didn't want this moment to end, this fairy-tale holiday romance that was so far removed from normality it didn't seem real—or possible.

'I don't think you can beat that,' she teased, the champagne making her head light, making any inhibitions she had slip away like the sun. As they'd dined with the soft sound of the waves close by Marco had raised a toast to her once more, just like their first night, and just like that first night she'd wanted so much more.

'Is that a challenge, Imogen?' His voice was soft

and seductive as he stopped and took her in his arms. She looked up into his face, searching his eyes, seeing nothing but desire and passion—for her. It made her feel special, alive, but more than anything it made her feel desired.

He lowered his head and his lips claimed hers, sending a shock wave of need hurtling through her. She wrapped her arms around his neck, sliding her fingers into his thick, dark hair as his hands slid over the silk of the dress she'd asked Julie to buy on her behalf, not caring of the cost, wanting only to be who she wasn't, who she could never be, for one more night.

His caress moved lower until he cupped her bottom, bringing her against the hardness of his erection, making her shudder and drag in a deep breath of pleasure. She didn't know how much longer she could play this game of seduction. All she wanted was him. All of him.

'Marco.' She breathed his name against his lips as he ended the kiss, still holding her intimately close. 'I want more than this. Much more.'

She shocked herself as her admission slipped wantonly from her. She'd never been the one to initiate things between her and Gavin, never been the seductress, but something about Marco made her feel different. It was that strange sensation that they were meant to be here, doing this, that they were destined to find each other. Or was that her incurable romantic side getting the better of her, finally resurfacing after the utter indignation of being left standing, practically at the altar?

'Since the night we met, I've wanted to make love

to you.' The deep, hoarse notes of his voice betrayed the desire he had been keeping control of, sending sparks of anticipation through her. She had never wanted a man the way she wanted Marco. This ultimate fantasy *had* to play out tonight—right to the very end. She couldn't return to her life and wonder what might have been. She wanted to take with her something special to cherish in her memory.

'I want that too, Marco. Tonight.' She looked up at him from lowered lashes, shy at such an admission.

In answer he kissed her, deeply and passionately, the soft swish of the waves blending with the thumping of her heart as his tongue plunged deep into her mouth, forcing a sigh of pleasure to rush from her. The kiss became frantic and wild as he held her head between his hands, keeping her exactly where he wanted her, where she wanted to be, so he could plunder her lips, ravish her mouth with such delicious control. Her whole body was on fire and she trembled as he let her go, holding her away from him as if he thought they would both lose control at any moment.

His gaze raked down over her body, lingering on her breasts as she breathed deep and hard with unquenched desire. She watched him, waiting for his next move in this desire-filled game he'd started.

'I want you, Imogen.' The guttural growl of his words left her in no doubt he was fighting hard to remain in control, forcing himself to hold back now. The idea that she'd done that to him, that he wanted her so much, only intensified her need for him.

'And I want you,' she whispered as he moved closer to her, putting his hand behind her head and bringing her close, pressing his forehead gently against hers as if they were truly lovers instead of a couple about to bring their holiday romance to a spectacularly passionate ending.

His kiss this time was soft, gentle, caressing. Any last reservations that she could actually go through with this and spend a night with a man she knew very little about vanished. Swept away by the passion and desire which was so real they could be lovers, real lovers.

Without another word he took her hand and led her along the beach. The star-filled sky and the rising moon lit the way, reflecting on the ocean as it lapped seductively at the shore. Each step she took was a step nearer to the moment she'd wanted since she'd first made eye contact with this sexy Italian New Yorker. Then she had been trying so hard not to be Imogen Fraser, assistant at Bespoke Luxury Travel. When he'd asked her name he'd sealed her fate, setting her free to be *just* Imogen, and even the fact that he didn't want to volunteer anything more about himself only added to the dream, the escape of the moment.

By tomorrow evening all this would be a dream and she and Julie would be back in England, back to the reality of their normal lives. That thought was driving her on, making her want this moment all the more. She'd never forgive herself if she stood in her own way of enjoying the fantasy of this last night. Something like this was hardly likely to happen to her again.

'This is where we will spend the night.' He stopped and she looked across the beach, to a cabana with white curtains drawn back and moving gently in the warm breeze. The lanterns beside the thatched cabana cast a romantic yellow glow. 'We can relax, enjoy the warmth of the night and watch the stars.'

What could be more romantic? 'All night?' She turned to him, a wicked desire to tempt him still further rushing through her.

'All night. And when we have seen enough of the magic of the sky we will close the curtains and be totally alone.'

'What if someone passes by?' The last thing she wanted was to have someone come along and spoil her fantasy night.

'There is nobody else on this part of the island. It's totally private, and now all the staff have gone, and we are completely alone.'

She smiled and moved towards the cabana, noticing the bucket of champagne cooling, wondering if she should indulge in any more. She was already losing her inhibitions, already losing her head and quite possibly her heart to a man she would never see again.

For a split second she wanted more than tonight, more than this magical moment. Then she remembered who she really was, that tomorrow *just* Imogen would no longer exist. And she knew that Marco would never look her way if he knew who she really was. The man was so far out of her league.

'You really have bought into the romantic escape.' Her voice was light and carefree as she tried to stamp out those dark thoughts and bring the desire-filled emotion back to her heart. She stepped under the thatched roof of the cabana and trailed her fingers along the white double bed from which they would look out to sea as they lay together. She stood and took in the view. Never had she imagined anything like this; it was totally surreal and hopelessly romantic.

Marco came close behind her, wrapping his arms around her waist, pulling her back against him. Passion was in every word as he whispered in her ear, sending a tingle of hot, sparking need down her spine. 'Whatever I do, I make sure it is the best.'

He kissed her neck and she sighed softly, leaning her head back against him, turning towards his face. 'Is that a promise?'

Who was this woman? What had happened to sensible Imogen Fraser? This escapism fantasy was definitely going to her head.

Before she could answer those questions as they rambled through her mind, he turned her quickly in his arms to face him. He didn't speak, but his deep and rapid breaths told their own story.

She looked up into his eyes, saw the swirling passion and hot desire in them. Slowly she went on tiptoes and teased a kiss on his lips. His hand skimmed down her back until he held her closer as he kissed her. The gentleness of that kiss soon gave way to hot, fiery passion as the dam finally burst. There would be no holding anything back now. She wanted nothing more than this moment with Marco.

'Marco,' she whispered as he kissed down her neck, this time going lower, down to her breasts. She closed her eyes against the wild, passionate heat his kiss brought to them. When his mouth closed over her nipple through the flimsy black silk of the dress she gasped in shock, pushing her fingers into his hair, holding him there.

She could hardly stand. Her knees were so weak

her legs wouldn't hold her much longer, and as if he knew the effect he was having on her he pushed her back onto the softness of the bed.

Without taking her gaze from his, she slid backwards further onto the bed, her breathing deep and fast. He removed his jacket, tossing it on the sand, then his bow tie and then his white shirt.

The sight of his firm, muscled chest only heightened her desire and the dark trail of hair arrowing downwards was almost too much. She pushed one of her heeled sandals off, then the other as he towered over her. For a moment he held her gaze before turning to close the curtains at the sides, leaving only the end looking out to sea, which gleamed silver, lit by the full moon.

Not that she cared much for the view right now. The only view she wanted to see was this man, this incredibly sexy man.

He moved back to the bed and placed his hand on her ankles, looking at her intently as his chest heaved with passion-induced deep breaths. Slowly he slid his hands up her legs, up under the hem of her dress, pushing it higher. She could barely take it as his fingers hooked into either side of the black lace panties.

He began to pull them down and she raised herself, wanting them gone, wanting all her clothing gone— and his.

This was the moment the whole week had been building towards. As if there was an unspoken agreement between them they'd courted one another, teased with light kisses, but never anything more. It was as if they had both known the outcome of the week on this paradise island from the moment they had first seen each other.

Imogen trembled with need as Marco looked down at her, but instead of removing the remainder of her clothing he knelt between her legs, then, with a quirk of his brow and a mischievous grin, pushed back the silk of her dress and kissed a trail from her bellybutton down. Her hands gripped at the bed as the trail of kisses went to the heated core of need only he could satisfy. She let her head fall back against the bed, unable to watch him as the ecstasy of his kisses swept her further away from reality, deeper into the fantasy.

He grasped her thighs as he kissed her intimately, almost sending her over the edge. She couldn't take much more and writhed away from him, wanting the moment to go on longer. He stopped and she lay there breathing rapidly, opening her eyes and looking up at the inside of the thatched roof, lit with small heart-shaped lights.

She raised her head and looked down at him when he moved away from her and she drew in a sharp breath when she saw him strip off the last of his clothes, leaving him beautifully naked and wonderfully aroused. She couldn't think straight any more, didn't want to. All she wanted was this man inside her—deep inside her. The fire of passion he'd just lit couldn't be extinguished now.

She watched, unable to help herself, as he rolled on a condom then moved over her, the intent in his eyes making them almost black. She felt his nakedness, his skin against her thighs, and wished she didn't still have her dress on. His body covered hers, pressing her into the bed, and the sexual tension she'd been battling with all week exploded. She wrapped her legs around him, following an instinct she had no idea she possessed. The heated hardness of his erection nudged at her, teasing her. But it wasn't enough. She wanted more. She lifted herself up, wanting him. All of him.

The muscles in his arms were rigid as he braced himself over her, looking down, as she moved and teased him. Reality was far away as she twisted against him, teasing him, begging him with her body to finish what he'd started.

He kissed her, hard and demanding, and she matched his passion, pulling him against her with her arms and her legs, wanting it all, wanting it now. The fever of the passion built as his kiss bruised her lips, their heavy breaths drowning out the sound of the waves. Still it wasn't enough. Still she wanted more, and she moved her hips as she writhed beneath him, wanting him inside her, filling her. With a feral growl of passion he pushed into her, deep and hard, sending stars of desire surging to join those looking down on them from the velvety sky.

It was wild. Passionate. It was everything and more than she'd wanted this night, their moment of true escape, to be.

He kissed her face as she gasped, then his lips claimed hers as he moved deep within her. She moved with him as he struck up a rhythm of passionate need, harder and deeper. He lifted his head up, bracing himself away from her again as he thrust deeper still. She clung to his shoulders as the pace became a frenzy of desire-induced need so wildly passionate. She moved with him, the moment so intense that nothing else mattered.

With a gasp of pleasure her body shook as stars burst behind her closed eyelids. Marco thrust once more, a wild growl tearing from him as he too gave himself up to the pleasure of the moment, his body shaking as he lay heavy on top of her.

Imogen clung to him as she slowly came back to earth, the sound of the waves gradually able to be heard once more. Her whole body was alive with desire, aware of the heat of his as he lay on her, breathing hard as he too returned from the ecstasy of what they'd just shared.

Marco lay next to Imogen as she slept, the sound of the waves welcoming the new day, heralding the end of their time together. Last night had been like no other he'd ever known. They'd made love again and then one final time in the early hours, as wildly and recklessly as the first time. But now it was time to leave the island, leave the escape this woman had provided.

The buzz of his mobile dragged him from the lust-inducing thoughts of last night. Even the moment when the condom had come off during that last wild coming together hadn't killed the passion. He hadn't been able to stop himself as they'd taken one another to the heights of dizzy passion until they could only lie exhausted and listen to the waves.

His phone sounded again, and he slipped off the bed, pulling on the trousers he'd discarded in a hurry last night before picking up his jacket and searching in the pocket for his mobile.

The text from his sister slammed reality back into him.

Father really ill. You are needed in New York. Call me.

He pulled on his shirt and walked out onto the beach as the pink hues of early morning were filling the sky. Standing looking out at the waves, he dialled and waited for it to connect. His sister's relief was obvious, and he listened to the update on his father's health. He turned to walk along the beach and looked up at the cabana. Imogen stood there, her black dress covering her body once more, a look of concern on her face. He ended the call and walked towards her. It was what they'd planned, what they'd both wanted, but he wasn't ready yet to end the fantasy of the last week.

He didn't want to go back to New York. He'd come here to escape from his mother's revelation of who he really was, finally able to understand why he'd never fitted in with his family, why he'd never been able to please his father, no matter what he'd done.

But he couldn't stay here. Imogen had her life, whatever that was, and he had his. It was time to end this. Time to return to reality and for him to face the harshness of it head-on.

'Problems?' Imogen's voice was cautious, her hair ruffled and her mouth bruised, telling a story of their passion. Lust stabbed at him once more and he wrestled with the idea of taking her back to bed one last time.

'My father is ill. I have to go back to New York immediately.'

She hugged her arms around her body as if she were cold, even though the heat of the day was already rising. 'Then you should go.'

He picked up his jacket and put it around her shoulders, not missing the way she tensed. 'I will take you back first.'

She looked at him, her eyes bluer than the ocean. 'Thank you for a wonderful week of escape.'

He was taken aback. He was expecting something more along the lines of *Call me*. But this was *just* Imogen, the woman who had made it abundantly clear that nothing else would ever happen between them once they had left the paradise of this island behind. It was exactly what he wanted. They'd quenched their desire for each other and now it was time to go back to their real lives.

He kissed her gently on the forehead, forcing himself to follow her detached example. 'Thank you.' He wasn't sure if it was for making a swift departure easier or for last night.

She pulled back from him, already creating distance. 'We'd better get going.'

She didn't say anything during their ride back to her villa, but once she'd stepped out of the small utility vehicle she turned to him. 'I hope your father is okay.'

'Thank you,' he said curtly, not liking the intrusion his father was having on this moment.

Slowly she handed him his jacket. 'Goodbye,

Marco.' Without another word she turned and walked away. He watched as she went into the villa, pausing at the door. She held his gaze across the expanding distance and smiled, before she went inside and closed the door, shutting him out of her life for good.

CHAPTER FOUR

Almost five months later

IMOGEN PLACED HER hand over the soft swell of her tummy and tried not to think of Marco, the man she'd escaped from reality with on the paradise island. The man who, as the father of her baby, had a right to know their week together had left a lasting legacy. For the last month, since she'd confided in Julie about the pregnancy, her friend had been wearing her down with her insistence that she find Marco.

She now accepted Julie was right, but knew also that the news would not be welcomed by Marco. He'd made it clear he wanted nothing more than their week of escape, something she had been more than happy to go along with. But now the man she knew only as Marco had to be found, and she had to tell him her news and prepare herself for his reaction.

Imogen pushed those thoughts to the back of her mind; her head was far too fuzzy and numb and she needed her wits about her today. After a lot of time off recently, claiming it to be a stomach bug instead of morning sickness, she had to be on top form, and trying to work out how to find Marco and give him the news about the baby wouldn't help her do that. Especially not right now, when Bespoke Luxury Travel was due to sign up their newest account, Silviano Leisure Group. Imogen berated herself for not having done her usual pre-meeting research on the company or its CEO, the man they were about to meet. The jewel in their crown, Silviano Leisure Group was a global company with high-end luxury destinations, including the island Julie and Imogen had been sent to.

How could she tell anyone anything about the island when to her it had become her escape? The romance of the island had become the place she'd lived the dream of love and happy-ever-after for one week. It was the place she'd experienced the most magical night of her life with a man she knew only as Marco. A man she'd known even then she'd never see again.

She touched her tummy once more; the legacy of that week of fantasy had grown startlingly real with each passing day since she'd done first one pregnancy test then another. She'd refused to believe it was possible until the morning sickness had started. It was only a month ago she'd had the courage to confide in Julie, who'd been on a mission ever since to track down Marco. A task more difficult than it seemed when neither of them knew hardly anything about him.

'Immy! Immy!' Julie burst into her office and Imogen couldn't decide if this was going to be good or bad news. She really didn't want any of Julie's well-meant but constant advice about finding Marco now. He'd made it clear their week would be just that. He hadn't wanted anything more from her, just as she hadn't from him. It should have been the perfect moment out of time, and it had been. The legacy of that moment, the baby she carried, was something she was finally beginning to come to terms with. He on the other hand could dismiss her claim as easily as he'd walked away that last morning.

'I think you should sit down,' Julie said, her breathing fast as if she'd just run up the two flights of stairs from Reception.

'What is it this time?' Imogen sat at her desk, hardly able to bring any energy into her words. Her mind was still reeling with all the implications of the situation she was now in. A single mother was not something she'd ever envisaged for herself, but she would get through it and shower her baby with so much love. And she had the support of her parents, a constant in her life.

'I've found him.' Julie's words rushed out.

'Who?'

'Marco, of course.'

'I haven't got time for this now, Julie. Mr Silviano is due any moment. I haven't done any preparation and we have a meeting to attend with him and our own CEO. This contract is big, Julie.' Imogen got up and walked round to the front of her desk.

'That's just it. He's here.' Julie looked at her as if begging her to understand. 'Marco is here.'

A sense of dread slipped down Imogen's spine. Marco was here? Things just couldn't get any worse. 'Marco is here?'

'Yes. You've only been and slept with the CEO of Silviano Leisure Group!' Imogen could hardly think, let alone breathe, as Julie's disbelieving words sank in.

'Marco? From the island?' Imogen whispered the words, as if it made it less real that way. 'That can't be right. You must have made a mistake.'

'It's no mistake, Immy. Marco, *your* Marco, is the CEO of Silviano Leisure Group. The father of your baby is New York billionaire businessman Marco Silviano.'

'No, no, it can't be.' Imogen couldn't think straight. He hadn't once said during their week on the island that he *owned* it. She shook her head in silent denial as her mind rushed back to that last night, to the lengths he'd gone to in ensuring they were alone. A guest couldn't have organised all that. Could he?

'Immy, it *is* him. I've seen him myself.' Julie clutched at her arm, imploring her to believe what she was saying.

'What? You saw him?' Imogen gasped as her heart began to pound. What would he think when he found out she wasn't the socialite she'd led him to believe, that she was just a member of staff at Bespoke Leisure Travel and had been sent to the island so that she could personally recommend it to their clients?

'Yes,' Julie said, exasperation filling the word.

'Did he see you?' The tentative question slipped from Imogen's lips as she tried to think how she was going to get out of this meeting. She couldn't see Marco. Not only would he discover who she was but if he had even the smallest amount of observation skills he would see she was pregnant.

Would he even think the baby was his? They had used condoms that night, although he should remember there had been that one moment the last time they'd made love. Would he even consider that it could have resulted in a baby? She doubted it. He was the kind of man who took his pleasure where he could and then moved on. She'd been well aware of that, but it had only made the escapism all the more appealing. A girl like her had caught the attention of a man like him.

'I can't do this. I can't see him.' Imogen pulled at her ponytail, racking her mind for what to do. 'Neither can you. If he recognises you then that's it.'

'You have to tell him about the baby, Immy.'

'No, we were only having a brief fling. There is no way I can tell him now—here.'

Imogen turned and walked to the window of her office, looking out over postcard-pretty Oxford. She thought back to the telephone call Marco had made that last morning on the beach, claiming his father was ill. She'd been convinced it was a way to ensure she left quietly and without any clinging requests to see him again, and she had done just that with as much dignity as she could. It had hurt, but she'd accepted on the very first night that they could never really be together, that they were from two different worlds. Even that tender and passionate night, which had been the closest she'd ever felt to being loved, hadn't made her want more. Now, knowing that night they had created a baby—their baby—she still didn't have any illusions there would be declarations of love and happy-ever-afters.

This was reality.

Marco had stepped from the fantasy of her memories and was here in her world—her reality. 'I can't see him, Julie, and I can't tell him.'

Her head began to thump as tension increased. Whatever was she going to do?

'You have to see Marco, Immy,' Julie said sympathetically as she came to stand next to her, both looking out over Oxford as if it held the solution to the problem. 'You should tell him.'

'What do I say?' Anger filled Imogen now as the scenario rushed through her mind. 'Pleased to meet you, Mr Silviano, and by the way, you are the father of my baby?'

'That's some introduction.' Marco couldn't understand how he'd kept his voice so calm when within the last few seconds he'd discovered not one, but two major revelations. He'd been in Reception and had been informed that Julie Masters and Imogen Fraser would see him shortly. The names had been like a slap in the face, then he'd seen Julie as she'd dashed back upstairs. He hadn't waited but had followed her up and hadn't missed a word of what Imogen had said.

The woman he'd shared a perfect week of escape with on his island hadn't left his mind since and a search on the internet for socialites named Imogen living in London had drawn a blank. None of them was anything like the blonde he'd had the hottest night of his life with. He had no idea why he wanted to see her again, why he'd even tried to find her, other than that he still had the need to escape his family, to rediscover the solace her glorious body had brought him.

Now he'd stumbled across her in the most unexpected way and the amusement at catching Imogen and Julie talking as they'd looked out of the office window had swiftly been replaced by shock as Imogen had spoken her last words. It was far more than the fact that *just* Imogen, wasn't the socialite she'd led him to believe. It was the shock that she claimed to be expecting a baby—his baby.

He thought back to their night of passion and the last time they'd enjoyed the pleasure of one another's bodies, to the moment when the condom had let him down. Was it really possible those few seconds had been enough to create the child he'd never wanted but had been consistently reminded by his mother and father that he needed?

Imogen turned around very slowly, as if the action would make him vanish, and he raised his brow in expectation of an explanation. It might not be the news he'd wanted to hear, but if what she said was true he knew he would do what was expected of him. Not just for Imogen and the baby's sake, but because it would be exactly what his grandfather would have wanted him to do. He'd always towed the line when his grandfather set the rules and, despite having lost him six years ago, he still liked to be guided by thoughts of his wisdom.

'Is it true?' Marco demanded, a little too hotly if the look on Imogen's face was anything to go by.

'Of course it is.' Julie leapt to her friend's defence, but he didn't take his eyes from Imogen's pale face. She still seemed incapable of saying anything.

'I think, Julie,' she finally managed in almost a whisper, her gaze locked defiantly with his, contradicting the weariness of her face, 'I think this is between me and Marco.'

He stepped fully into the office and stood by the

open door, waiting for Julie to leave them alone. This was not the meeting he'd come here for today. Never in his wildest dreams had he imagined that *just* Imogen and Imogen Fraser were one and the same. And he certainly hadn't anticipated her startling revelation.

Julie glared at him as she left the office and he wouldn't mind betting she'd love to give him a piece of her mind. As the door closed, somewhat noisily, behind her he watched as Imogen moved away from the shield the back of her desk chair had offered.

His attention was drawn to her stomach, to the way the buttons on the blouse were pulled tight over the swell of her tummy and the way the fabric strained across her now much fuller breasts.

He sighed and pressed his thumb to his chin, rubbing his fingers over the other side of his face, feeling the sharpness of new stubble. His week of escape had a permanent hold on him. A consequence there was no escaping from. He was going to be a father.

'I'm sorry, Marco,' Imogen said as she walked towards him, her chin lifting in determination with each step. 'I didn't want you to find out like this.'

'So what were you going to do? Drop it casually into the agenda of the meeting?'

'That's not fair.' She railed against his sarcasm. 'I didn't even know it was you until a few minutes ago!'

'Didn't know it was me?' She wasn't making much sense. Either that or his mind had gone to mush.

'When we said goodbye on the island all I knew about you was that you lived in New York and your first name was Marco. I certainly didn't know who the CEO of Silviano Leisure Group was.' Her indignation showed as clearly as her desire had the night he'd kissed her on the beach before he'd taken her to the cabana for the hottest night of sex he'd ever had. 'I had no reason to think the Marco I met on the island was Marco Silviano.'

She turned quickly from him, pressing her fingertips to her forehead and going to her desk chair, flopping down wearily in it. A spike of guilt at taunting her shot through him, swiftly followed by concern.

'Are you okay?' He went behind her desk, forcing her to look up at him as he stood at her side.

'Perfectly,' she snapped and picked up a file, hugging it against her breasts as if trying to conceal the shocking truth of the baby that grew inside her. 'And for the record, I expect nothing from you. Nothing at all.'

'Is that so?' He leant back against her desk, his arms folded across his chest as he looked down at her. 'And by nothing you mean that I should simply walk away and allow you to bring my child up alone?'

'Precisely.' She clutched the file tighter. Amusement filtered through him. Imogen Fraser was far more prickly than *just* Imogen, and for some reason, despite what he'd just learnt, he liked the challenge she now threw at him.

'Where? Here in Oxford or at Daddy's house in London?' He couldn't help but taunt her again, knowing full well why she'd gone along with Julie's suggestion, and he was under no illusion just who it was who'd fabricated the whole story. 'And what with? Daddy's fortune?'

'I'm perfectly capable of bringing up my baby.' The response flew at him like a dart.

He took the file from her and placed it on the desk,

his calm and slow movements silencing her protest. 'My child will be brought up in New York.'

He had no idea where that had come from other than that it was what his grandfather would have expected him to do. When he'd walked in here this afternoon he hadn't anticipated coming face to face with Imogen and most certainly not with the news that he was to be a father, the one thing he'd vowed he'd never be. A child was the last thing he wanted. However, the reality was different. A child was now exactly what he *needed*.

'What? Why?' Imogen hurled the words at him.

'I wish to provide everything my child needs.' Marriage and parenthood had never been on his agenda—he'd avoided them at all costs. Now Imogen, the only woman to have come close to crashing through his protective wall, was carrying his child. A son or daughter that would end his mother's constant demands on him to provide an heir—and as much as it pained him to admit, Marco knew if the baby was a boy, he could satisfy his father's old-fashioned views and prove himself worthy of his respect...his love.

Imogen shook her head, slowly at first, then faster. 'How are you going to manage that? I have no intention of going to New York and you certainly can't force me to.'

Panic raced through her, making her feel so dizzy she couldn't stand up and face him. She might well have been in denial for the last few months, trying to avoid admitting that the wonderfully romantic night she'd spent in Marco's arms had created a baby, but right now she felt incredibly protective of the new life inside her. A lasting legacy of one night of passion.

'I have no intention of forcing you to do anything.' He spoke firmly as he paced across the room towards the door. Her panic levels notched up. Was he about to walk out on her? She took a deep, calming breath as he turned and paced back towards her, stopping next to the desk and looking out of the window. 'I want what's best for you and the baby, but my business dictates I am based in New York. There I can give you both a lifestyle that will mean neither of you will ever want for anything. I can give you the kind of security you and the baby deserve.'

She stood up quickly, a little too quickly if the spinning of her head was anything to go by. She looked at his profile, at the firm set of his mouth, and wondered where the Marco she'd spent that week with had gone. This Marco was the hard-edged businessman she'd always known he was—she just hadn't known what business that was and certainly hadn't expected to come face to face with him again as part of her job.

'You seriously expect me to go to New York?' Her words were a croaky whisper, giving away just how scared she really was at this moment.

'Yes. I want my child to be born there, to grow up there.' He spoke without looking at her, as if she was inconsequential against what he wanted.

'To live there?'

'It's not such a difficult concept.' Marco said without looking at her.

'That's where you are wrong.' Imogen finally found her strength, her will to fight. 'You can't just charge back into my life and demand that I leave my family behind and go to New York with you.'

Imogen had only recently explained to her mother and father about the baby. They'd been shocked, but, with the unwavering support they'd offered her all her life, they'd told her they would help her. They'd even suggested that she could return to live with them in the countryside surrounding Oxford if she needed to. How would they feel if she left for New York—with a man she barely knew?

Marco turned to face her, his eyes dark and unfathomable. His lips pressed together into a determined line and she couldn't help remembering the pleasure they'd given as he'd kissed her. Not that there was any trace of desire or passion on his handsome face now.

'As I said, it is not such a difficult concept. You are expecting my baby, are you not?'

Imogen swallowed hard. 'Yes, I am, but if you doubt that, if you for one minute do not believe me, then walk away right now.'

She lifted her chin, straightened her spine, injecting strength she hadn't known she possessed into her words. Just who did he think he was to come in here and demand she leave everyone and everything behind that she held dear?

His gaze locked with hers and she knew instantly that walking away was not something this man did. She'd issued him a challenge and he was going to take it on no matter what. He moved closer to her. Too close, as the scent of his aftershave opened up powerful memories of their time together on the island.

'I don't doubt that the child you carry is mine.' His tone had gentled, lulling her into a false sense of security. 'Neither do I expect you to turn your back on your life here.'

'How can I not, when you expect me to move halfway around the world and give up everything? My job, friends, family?'

He moved a little closer, his expression intense. 'You can have the pick of any job in my company, and your family and friends can visit you often. I also have a house in London and you may go there whenever you wish. A move would require changes, but not sacrifices.'

'I just don't know what it would do to my parents if I moved away, if I went to live in New York...' She shook her head in disbelief as the sentence trailed off.

She'd had the perfect upbringing, been the much-loved and only daughter, and although they had never been well off she hadn't gone without anything she needed. She just couldn't turn her back on that, on her parents. For her, family was everything.

'You have strong family connections?' His voice hardened and became laced with suspicion.

'Yes, I do.' Imogen defended her family, his question feeling more like an attack, especially after their time on the island. He'd rushed to his father's bedside and she assumed it meant family was important to him too.

'And what of your new family?' he demanded.

He moved one step closer and as she looked up at him she couldn't help thinking of the time she'd wound her arms around his neck, plunged her fingers into his thick, dark hair and kissed him as if her life had depended on it. Annoyed at the pulse of desire which began deep inside her, she pushed the memory away. It didn't belong with the Marco who stood in front of her now.

'My new family?' She tried to process his question, tried to understand what he meant.

'Our family. You, me and the baby. Us.'

'We're not a family.' She stepped back away from him, trying to lessen the thudding of her heart, the heat of need for this man. It was as if he was talking in code, or a foreign language she only understood bits of.

'We will be, Imogen.' He smiled at her, but it didn't quite reach his eyes.

'What are you saying, Marco? Because it seems to me that you are trying to make me feel guilty, trying to test my loyalty to my parents against my love for my baby.'

He took her hands in his and for a moment Imogen was back on the island, where she'd spent a week without a care in the world. She was back with the kind and considerate Marco who'd treated her like a princess and made her feel more special than anyone had ever done.

'I want *us* to be a family, Imogen.'

Had her memories played havoc with her ability to hear correctly? Had they made her believe her deepest desire had come true? Marco wanted her. He wanted the baby and, more than that, he wanted them to be a family.

'You want us to be a family?' She whispered the question at him as she searched his eyes, searched their depths for the man she'd met five months ago.

'You have what I need, and I can provide you with all you could want.'

Those last words jarred in her thoughts, reminding her of the predicament she was in, but it was his less than romantic declaration which had jolted her from her fantasy of Marco, the handsome man she'd had a holiday romance with, a week of total escape. She looked into his face, into his eyes, and saw nothing but cold determination.

'I think you had better explain that reasoning, because what you've just said certainly isn't going to make me say anything other than no.'

Marco looked at Imogen and knew he'd made a mistake. His snap decision to turn the news he'd just learnt into something that would solve his problems as well as Imogen's hadn't played out in the way he'd imagined it would.

'The baby…' He paused and tried again. '*Our* baby would continue my family name and, whilst being a father is not what I had planned, I will do my duty. I want our baby.'

As he said those words he knew it was true. He did want his baby, and he wanted to be very much part of its life. He wanted to try and be the kind of father he'd never known. He wanted to slam the door on his past shut once and for all.

She bit her lower lip, frowning at him in suspicion. 'You really want our baby? To be part of its upbringing?'

He took advantage of her moment of doubt and brushed the backs of his fingers across her face. 'Yes, Imogen. I want our baby, the baby we created that night on the island.'

He could see her again in his mind, abandoned to

the pleasure of his touch, his kiss. He had no doubt it had been as wildly erotic for her as it had been for him. He wanted to be like that again with Imogen. The need was so far removed from what he'd always believed he wanted, he couldn't yet completely understand it.

'We can't both bring up the baby, not when we live on opposite sides of the world.'

As Imogen spoke, his mind raced with the possibility that finding out he was to be a father was the best thing that could have happened. The fact that Imogen was the mother, the woman he'd created that baby with, was even better. Despite neither of them being honest about who they were that week, it had been the week he'd been able to let go and be himself.

Everything had happened so fast. Less than an hour ago he'd been in the back of the limo being driven from London to Oxford. He'd just received the latest update on his father's health from his sister and knew things were not looking good, that his medication hadn't yet proved successful. He'd tried to feel some empathy for the man he'd believed to be his father all his life, the man he'd never been able to please, no matter what.

Now he knew why, and as he'd looked into Imogen's pale face, seen the fear and trepidation as she'd confirmed she was carrying his child, he had an inkling of how Emilio, the man he'd always referred to as his father, must have felt. Emilio had known the child his fiancée—Marco's mother, Mirella—carried could be his own brother's, after their affair had come to light the night his brother had been killed in a road accident. Emilio had married Marco's mother and claimed the baby as his, despite the truth that was revealed after the birth—and kept it secret from Marco until very recently.

Marco had no doubt the child Imogen carried was his, but his child had to be born a Silviano. This was his chance to find a way to finally please his family, to not be that disappointment his father had had to bear all these years.

'We don't *have* to live on opposite sides of the world, Imogen. Not if we get married.' The words came slowly and purposefully from him, so calm, so emotionless, he briefly wondered if he'd actually said them aloud.

'Married? You want us to get married?' Imogen's words confirmed he had spoken aloud. He had done the one thing he'd strived not to do all his adult life: ask a woman to marry him.

'I want to be part of my child's life. The child will always keep our lives entwined, and marriage would give us all more security.' He let those words sink in, hoped they sounded romantic and genuine, hoped they would convince her that marriage was the best solution to the situation they now found themselves in. Surely if she valued family so much she wouldn't want to be a single mother.

'More *security*?' The question in her voice made him realise she wanted more—deserved more. They had shared something special on the island and because of that Imogen deserved the truth.

'The morning we left the island I had a call.' He paused, seeing again Imogen standing beside the cabana as the sun had risen, her black evening dress looking sexier than ever in the dawn light. In that moment he'd wanted to stay locked away with her for ever, but the reality of his family life had intruded. He'd known he had to return to New York and do his duty, please his family. Then as his father's health had rallied after the heart bypass operation he'd deferred the need to take life seriously, throwing himself into his work—and his leisure.

'Yes—your father? Is he okay?' She gasped, looking concerned and confused at the same time.

She remembered? It jolted him sharply, as did the concern in her eyes, the way she moved towards him, reaching out as if wanting to offer comfort.

'Marco? Your father?' she prompted, as his thoughts prevented him from continuing with the truth she had to know.

'He is very ill. He had a triple heart bypass soon after I returned from New York and all was well for a while. Now it seems he has developed blood clots in his lungs because of the surgery and only time will tell if medication can deal with it.'

She placed her hand on his arm and looked into his eyes. The honesty and compassion in hers made him feel like a fraud. It also cut him to the very core, made him feel totally inadequate. She seemed to care more about his father, a man she'd never met, than he did. But what else was he supposed to feel when his father had emotionally locked himself away all these years, been totally unreachable? For a split second he was that young boy again, desperate to gain his father's approval. Always failing. Always falling short of what a Silviano heir should be. He might well be a Silviano son, but now he knew that, as far as the man he'd thought of as a father was concerned, he was the wrong son. The wrong heir.

'I'm sorry, for you and your family. It must be hard, dealing with that and now finding out you are to be a father yourself.'

Even now, Imogen was thinking of him, of others, believing he and his family were close. He envied her innocence, her strong sense of family. It was coming through loud and clear as if she was proclaiming it at the top of her voice that family was everything to her. She truly belonged to hers. He didn't, even though he'd tried. He and Imogen were complete opposites. They had so little in common, yet fate had conspired to bring them together and link them inexplicably for ever.

'I was here on business anyway and am returning to New York this evening. It wasn't what I expected when I came here, but we can get through this together. After all, we made the baby together.'

Her hand slipped from his arm and she blushed at his reference to their night together. Then she looked down, her long lashes shielding the turmoil of emotions he'd just glimpsed in her eyes. 'It is, yes, but we can talk about it another time. You should go to your father, your family.'

'I want you to come too—as my fiancée, and mother-to-be of my child.'

She looked up at him slowly and all the emotion, all the pain he should be feeling right now was there in her eyes. 'But...?'

'I want my father to meet you, to know you carry his grandchild, his heir.'

'Do you really think it will make a difference to

him?' The honesty in her eyes as she looked up at him was almost too much.

'If what my sister tells me is correct, then it is possible there is limited time.' He skirted around the issue. After Imogen's revelation it was of paramount importance to take her to New York, to prove to his father and himself that he could at least get this right.

'If I go, it won't mean I have agreed to living in New York permanently, or to my baby being born there, and definitely not to us getting married, but your father is my baby's grandfather and that counts for something as far as I am concerned.'

He should tell her the truth, tell her that their baby now had the entire future of the Silviano family in its hands. Guilt crashed over him. Silviano tradition always favoured a baby boy being the first born, and his parents would be hoping for a boy. And no matter who his father was, *he* was still a Silviano.

But he pushed those negative thoughts aside and held her gently by her arms as she looked up at him, that connection they'd shared on the island so very close to the surface again, but this wasn't the time to allow passion and desire to have free rein. This was more like a business deal which needed careful handling. It wasn't what he'd intended when the plan had rapidly formed in his mind, but it was enough—for now.

'Thank you, Imogen.' He spoke firmly, as if he was in the boardroom of Bespoke Luxury Travel negoti-ating a deal instead of trying to persuade the mother of his child to come to New York with him. He would take what she offered—for now. Once in New York he would prove to her that marriage was the only option. 'I accept your terms.'

Imogen blinked in shock at the formality of his tone, the choice of his words, but he had to be like that, otherwise all that had been between them during their week of escape would return. It would drag his barriers down just as it had almost done then. It would open up the door to his emotions and right now that was the last thing he needed.

'You make it sound more like a business deal.' There was a hint of teasing mixed in with the confusion which was clear in her voice. 'But for my baby's grandfather's sake, I will go with you to New York—just for a while.'

'We will leave today for London. I'd like you to see a doctor first.'

'A doctor?' Suspicion laced the word.

'I simply want to ensure you and the baby are well to fly.'

'I saw my own doctor just two weeks ago. We are both fine.'

'You were not planning a long-haul flight to New York then. I told you I would look after you and the baby, Imogen, and I mean to start doing that right now.' He'd never known such a strong urge to protect, such a powerful need to care for someone. He hadn't been in Imogen's company for very long and already she was bringing out the Marco he'd spent his whole life hiding.

'There is no need. I am due to have another scan in a few weeks and I have already asked the doctor about flying, in case I needed to know for work, so that is fine.'

'Very good. Then we will fly out tonight.'

'You seriously expect me to just drop my life and go with you—today?'

'My car will take you to your home to collect whatever you need, and I will make all the necessary flight arrangements. And when I meet with your employer I will clear things here.' He looked at his watch. 'A meeting we are both now late for.'

'I'm not going to the meeting. Julie is giving my apologies, so you had better go.' Her flippant tone warned him she was far from onside in this deal they'd just struck. Was she urging him to go to the meeting so she could slip away? He dismissed that notion as soon as it came to him.

'Be ready to leave for London in two hours.' He wasn't used to his decisions being challenged and his tone was far sharper than he'd intended.

'Whatever happens, Marco, I want you to remember one thing: I'm not doing this for you, or even myself.' She stood her ground, an air of defiance radiating from her gorgeous body. 'I'm doing this for family. For my baby's family—your father.'

CHAPTER FIVE

DURING THE LONG flight to New York, Imogen had made good use of the time and space in First Class to think about all Marco had said. Before she'd left, she'd told her parents how happy she was that Marco had come back into her life and how they were going to visit his parents and tell them of the baby and their engagement. She had explained Marco's father's ill health as their need for haste and her mother and father had waved her off with big smiles, believing it was what she wanted, that she was happy. She'd even let Julie believe that all was okay between her and Marco and that they were going to make a go of it. The guilt at the lies had eaten away at her as the plane had flown further and further away from England.

Now as the elevator sped towards Marco's penthouse apartment she was on edge, wondering if agreeing to coming as his fiancée, to a city she'd always wanted to visit, had been the right thing to do. Not only for her, but also for Marco's family and even her family. More important than that, was it the right thing for her baby—their baby?

'Oh, my goodness.' The words rushed from her as she walked into the apartment, the distinct shape of the Empire State Building dominating the view of New York. Already the city's lights of early evening were beginning to sparkle. It was as if she'd stepped back into a world of escape. 'The view is amazing.'

'The view?' Marco frowned and looked at it. 'I suppose it is.'

'How can you not be in awe of such a view?' She couldn't help but tease him; the sense that none of this was real, as if they were the couple they had been on the island, was too strong.

He shrugged. 'I've seen it many times.' His dismissive tone brought her up sharp, making her acutely aware that they were as far from the couple they had been on the island as it was possible to be. They were so very different and it wasn't just that they were expectant parents; it was as if they'd both put up insurmountable barriers and were now fiercely protecting them.

She walked over to the floor-to-ceiling windows which spanned the entire width of the living area and looked out over the city that notoriously never slept. She'd always wanted to see it, always wanted to be here, but never in her wildest dreams had she thought her first experience of it would be from the luxury apartment of a man like Marco Silviano. A man so very different from her. A man whose world looked nothing like hers.

'How are we going to make this work?' The question slipped from her in a whisper as she spoke more to herself than Marco.

Marco moved to stand behind her, his hand resting on her shoulder. 'We worked before,' he said softly, his voice more reminiscent of the week they'd shared on the island, and she knew instantly how easy it would be for her to fall back to that moment, to believe it was real. If she did nothing else to protect herself, she had to remind herself of the deal he'd put to her as if he was merely negotiating a new contract.

She turned to face him, shocked when she found just how close he was, but it was the heavy darkness in his eyes, the unmistakable desire, which really shocked her. She couldn't deal with this, not after the way he'd asked her to come here as his fiancée, making it sound like a business deal. If she allowed herself to be lulled into a false sense of security by him now, allowed herself to be fooled into thinking he genuinely wanted her, she knew her heart was in grave danger of becoming his. The cold, hard fact was that if she hadn't been carrying his child, if he hadn't overheard her and Julie talking, they wouldn't be here together right now. That was something she needed to hold on to no matter what.

Imogen doubted he would even have recognised her in the compulsory navy skirt and jacket she wore at work instead of the designer dresses she'd worn during that week. People like her only existed to make the lives of people like him more comfortable, which was the harsh reality she was already well aware of. Men like Marco thought he could snap his fingers and get exactly what he wanted. The fact that he'd arranged for her to leave her job so easily, without any questions directed at her, made her well aware of that.

'We did, yes. But that wasn't real, Marco.' She wanted to step back from him to put up barriers, create some distance, but the desire in those dark eyes just made her long for the impossible. She wanted to kiss him, to be kissed by him. She wanted it to be like their week together, but it could never be like that. 'Neither of us wanted more from that week. We didn't even let each other know who we really were. It was an escape from reality for both of us.'

'But now we have more, Imogen.'

'No.' She shook her head hard and moved away from him, away from the temptation of drifting back into the fantasy they'd shared for such a brief time. 'We have nothing but a deal, Marco. I agreed to be here, to be your fiancée, the mother of your child, so that your father could know about the baby—because he is ill. That's all and I'm doing it for my baby, so that one day I can tell him or her that I met your family.'

He turned to look out of the windows. 'And if we are going to make it convincing then I should also provide you with an engagement ring.'

'That's not necessary.' She couldn't help the laughter which filled her voice, the only way she could deal with all this. 'I don't need an engagement ring.'

'My sister has already arranged an engagement party for us tomorrow night.'

'You've already told your family we are engaged?' Shock made her whirl round to face him.

'I have, yes, and you will need to be wearing my ring. Everyone will want to see the woman who has finally tamed Marco Silviano, I can assure you of that.'

'Everyone?' Nerves tore through her. This wasn't part of the deal. She'd had images of visiting a sick man in hospital, of meeting Marco's mother and maybe his sister, but not this. 'A big party?'

She paced across the open-plan living space and despite the vastness of the view felt confined. As if she'd been lured into a trap. How had everything got so out of hand?

'Yes, a big party. My sister doesn't know half-measures.' He turned to look at her and her heart flipped over when he smiled. It was a real smile. One that made his eyes sparkle, and memories of their fun-filled date on the last day on the island rushed back. 'I'd like to see you in that black dress again.'

Imogen blushed. He remembered what she'd worn the night they'd spent in the cabana on the beach. The soft, seductive tone of his voice left her in no doubt of that, but that dress had only just fitted her then. There was no way it would fit now. 'I'm afraid nothing I have with me is suitable for a party, even if it did fit.' She instinctively flattened her palm against the soft swell of her tummy, blushing again as Marco's attention went to where his baby was now beginning to make its presence obvious.

Marco watched as Imogen placed her hand over her stomach, over the small bump of his child growing inside her. A fierce streak of protectiveness crashed over him, just as it had when she'd moved out from behind the chair in her office, as if to prove her claim of carrying his child. He looked at her fingers splayed over the bump of his baby, the reality of it all sinking in deeper. Beneath her palm was his child. The child he would now do anything for. That unfamiliar truth settled over him and he knew that no matter what, he would do exactly that.

He pushed down that protectiveness as it threatened to unleash emotions he had no need for right now. 'In that case, if you are feeling well enough after the flight, we should shop for a ring and a dress.'

'I really don't think it's necessary.' She looked uncomfortable and, dressed in a casual, loose-fitting sweater over black leggings, she didn't look at all like the woman who had captured his attention in that blue silk creation which had showcased every delicious curve of her gorgeous figure. She looked vulnerable and very innocent. Even so, she still had the same effect on him, still filled his body with fiery need.

A dart of hot lust shot through him and he bit down on the need to satisfy it. He might be back in New York, back to his reality, but Imogen had never been part of that reality. She belonged in the erotic and hot dreams which had plagued him since he'd left the island. Or at least *just* Imogen did. Imogen Fraser, however, belonged very much in his reality now.

This Imogen was part of his future. A future he hadn't ever looked into, but now she was part of it he realised that becoming a father, a married man, was about far more than just pleasing his family.

'A ring is necessary, Imogen. You made your conditions and now I am making mine. You agreed to come here, to be my fiancée. Now you will accept from me everything I need to give you to convince my family this is real, whether that is a ring or a dress. No one must doubt our engagement, least of all my mother or father.' The word almost stuck in his throat.

If he was honest with himself, Marco knew he wasn't doing this just for his father. Or at least not the man he'd grown up thinking was his father. He was doing it for his grandfather, the man who had left Sicily to live in America with his new wife, where they had set up a coffee shop. Marco often wondered what his grandfather would think to know that his little coffee shop was the foundation of Silviano Leisure Group and something he'd strived to keep even when his father had tried to suggest it was part of the past, that it had no place in the company's future.

'I'm not sure I can go through with this.' Imogen moved away from the windows and sat down on the softness of the sofa. She looked weary. 'We hardly know each other.'

Marco remembered that last night with her, recalled the pleasure they'd given one another. 'I think you will find we know one another quite well.'

She gasped and blushed as his meaning became clear. 'That's not what I meant and you know it.' The reprimand in her voice made him laugh, which only served to make her blush deepen. He'd never known a woman who blushed so prettily, so genuinely.

He sat beside her, took one of her hands in his and looked into her face. The caution in her eyes reproached him and he knew he needed to be open with her, tell her everything about his family. 'Imogen, my father is a strict man and I fear I was not the easiest of children. At least, not like my younger sister.'

As Imogen's attention fixed on him he wasn't sure he was ready to tell her the whole truth yet. It shocked him to realise he was telling her anything about his family, something he'd never done with any other woman. In a way he didn't yet understand, Imogen had opened the door to his past, to his childhood, and also uncovered the hurt of the truth his mother had finally confessed to.

He was beginning to understand Imogen's remark about his father being her baby's grandfather. Guilt slashed at him again as he recalled how often he'd been harsh on his father, unaware of the truth. The knowledge that he'd been responsible for his parents' marriage initially being so rocky was hard to bear. If the man lying ill in hospital could raise another man's child, then there was no way he could turn his back on *his* child. Whatever kind of man his upbringing had shaped him to be, he wouldn't turn his back on Imogen or the baby. He wouldn't be as cold as his father.

'Are you trying to warn me that this little one—' she looked down at her tummy, again placing her hand on the small bump '—is going to be a whole lot of trouble just like his father?'

He laughed, thankful she had lightened the mood, thankful he hadn't spilt out the entire story of his past as if it was some kind of excuse for being the hard-edged businessman who'd never wanted to settle down. He'd just never met a woman who'd made him want that.

He let her hand go and went to stand at the window once more, the early-evening dusk almost gone now as the sky became darker. Slowly he turned to face Imogen, aware he should have made his plans much clearer from the outset, but he'd been so shocked at the discovery of Imogen, let alone pregnant Imogen, he hadn't handled things as he should have. He hadn't been his usual cool and in-control self.

'My family has become more and more insistent that I marry and produce the next Silviano heir to inherit.'

'I see.' She slowly stood up and hugged her arms

around herself as if cold—or was it a protective move? 'So what exactly are you expecting of me, Marco?'

'I want us to be married—before the baby is born. But I'm not being manipulated by family pressure and tradition. I want us to be married because this is my baby and I want it to be born a Silviano.'

Imogen's eyes widened and she opened her mouth as if to speak, but nothing came out. Then she sat back down, disbelief all over her face, and when she did look up at him there was sadness in her eyes and he hated that he was hurting her, upsetting her.

He couldn't go to her and hold her as he wanted to. If he did he'd be showing weak emotions and that was something he never did—except for a blissful week on a paradise island.

'You and the baby will want for nothing, Imogen.'

'You brought me here on the pretext of introducing me as your fiancée to make your seriously ill father happy that you had a child on the way. You accepted I wanted to return to England, that marriage wasn't part of the deal. Now you change all the rules, all the conditions and say we must be married?'

'I will be part of my child's upbringing, Imogen. Surely you can see that marriage will be the best way? That it will be best for all of us?' Marco bristled and defended himself.

'There is one thing I want, Marco, one thing my baby will want, and you haven't mentioned it once. Not once.' She looked tearful and he suddenly felt completely out of his depth.

'I have told you I will give you everything you both need.'

She shook her head slowly. 'Not everything, Marco. Your luxury lifestyle can't buy everything.'

He scowled at her. 'What do you mean?'

'I can't marry you just because we are having a baby.' Her voice implored him to understand, but he didn't. 'I can't even truly be your fiancée, although I will do what I agreed to in England and meet your father and mother, but after that I want to return home.'

'That makes no sense, Imogen. I am the baby's father.'

'And you will always be that. You can spend time with him or her whenever you want, but...' Her voice trailed off.

'But what?'

Imogen looked at Marco as he stood there, his tall, athletic body dominating the New York skyline behind him. Just a few moments ago she'd thought she'd seen the real Marco, the man he didn't want the world to see. She'd been wrong. The real Marco was this commanding man who dominated and dictated. The man who thought he could dangle the carrot of his lifestyle before her and make her do exactly what he wanted.

'What about love, Marco?' Her words had become a quiet whisper by the time she said his name, her voice frightened away by the severe expression the word 'love' had brought to his face.

'Love?' The word rushed from him like a bullet from a gun.

'Yes, Marco, love.'

'My reason for us to marry is because of our baby, not love.' He ground the words out as if they were poison, dashing any glimmer of hope she had that after their romantic week on the island they could find love.

'When I marry I want it to be for love.' Imogen tried to push aside the thought that she would never find a man to love her, the cruel taunts over her weight when she was a teenager surfacing rapidly, wiping away all the time she'd spent accepting herself for who she was. While all the other girls had had an endless stream of boyfriends she'd been at home studying, trying to pretend she didn't care. Even Gavin, who'd claimed he loved her, had left her and sought the company of glamorous, thin, model-like women.

'But you are pregnant with my baby.'

'This is the twenty-first century, Marco. That doesn't mean I *have* to marry you.'

She watched his brow furrow as he thought of what she'd said and bizarrely she wanted to laugh. The mighty CEO of Silviano Leisure Group had been reduced to confused silence—by her.

'I want to be a part of my child's life and marriage will give me the security that I can be, even if you insist we are on different sides of the world.'

'I'm sorry, Marco, but I've made my decision. Once I have done what I agreed to do, I am returning to England, not marrying you.'

'What else do you expect from me, Imogen?' His voice had sharpened, and she knew he was frustrated, but this was for the best. Soon enough he would forget her and move on to the next svelte woman. She'd be a fool to think this man was any different from Gavin.

'That's just it, Marco.' She stood up and walked towards him, desperate to make him see he didn't have to do any of this out of a sense of duty. The only way they could be together was if he loved her and, despite the romantic week they'd had on the island, she now knew without any doubt that love was not part of this man's life. 'I don't want or expect anything from you.'

'When I walked into the office you and Julie were talking—she was saying you had to tell me. You must have wanted something from me?'

'You don't know me at all if you think that.' Sadness filled her voice. 'I wanted you to know for the baby's sake. It's important to me that my child knows who his or her father is because family is everything. It's why I agreed to come here in the first place.'

'Then I must convince you that staying here in New York as my wife will be the best way to do that.' He turned from her. She had no idea if he was brooding over the view or calculating his next move. Either way, she had to make her decision clear to him.

'We can see your father tomorrow, then I'm going home.' She had to make him understand that a marriage like that was not what she wanted—for her *or* the baby.

He turned swiftly to her. 'You will stay until we have convinced my parents and my sister that we are serious about marriage, that we will be bringing up the baby as a Silviano.'

Imogen's emotions were all over the place. In fact, they had been since she'd returned from the island and she'd put that down to missing Marco, to having to end the escape they'd shared. Not for one minute had she thought it was due to being pregnant. Now those emotions were getting the better of her despite his cold attitude. She had to remind herself he was doing this for the baby, for its right to be a Silviano.

'Two weeks.' She injected as much firmness into her voice as possible. A tiny part of her heart hoped she and Marco might rediscover whatever it was that had brought them together in the first place, but once her head ruled again she knew that it had only been lust between them and not love.

'Two weeks?'

'Yes. I will be your fiancée for two weeks and then I will return to England.'

Marco looked at her, the darkness of his eyes fixed on her face. 'I *will* convince you that marriage is for the best, Imogen. That raising our child, here, together, is the only way.'

CHAPTER SIX

IMOGEN HAD WOKEN to sunlight streaming in through her bedroom window the next morning and briefly wondered where she was. The events of the last two days, since Marco had arrived at her office and overheard her and Julie talking, had played out all night in her dreams, the conclusions so vivid, so full of what she truly longed for, that right now she wasn't sure what was reality and what was wishful thinking on her part.

She'd walked around the vast apartment, wondering what she was expected to do, until she'd seen the note Marco had left propped against the coffee machine. The large, flowing handwriting had brought her slamming back to reality and the nausea she'd thought she'd finished suffering from rushed back as she read the words.

Gone into the office whilst you are catching up on sleep. Be ready at lunchtime.

She'd showered and dressed in a loose-fitting black dress, annoyed at herself for taking time and care on her make-up, as if that would make all the difference.

Marco wasn't about to fulfil the dreams she'd had last night and fall in love with her. Besides, after everything she'd been through with Gavin the last thing she wanted to do was put her heart on the line again.

Now she sat in a jewellery store in Manhattan and the whole thing seemed far *too* real. Spread before her was an array of rings, so expensive she shuddered at the thought of wearing any of them. She hadn't considered a ring when she'd agreed to come here as his fiancée and meet his mother and father, and even if she had it would never have been anything like one of these.

'I think this one,' Marco said as he gently took her hand and slipped onto her finger a large diamond set within an oval of smaller diamonds. It fitted as if it had been made for her and, whilst it was so very pretty, it was still a symbol of a deal he'd made with her because of circumstances. 'Perfect.'

He still held her hand as she looked at him, momentarily lost for words. Wearing his ring, the one he'd chosen and placed on her finger as if it really meant something, was so close to what she could so easily secretly hope for, if she let herself be fanciful, that saying anything was difficult. Finally, she found her voice. 'Does it have to be so big, so expensive?'

'It does.' He looked at her, his expression hard and businesslike, with not a trace of emotion. 'A ring like this gives a very clear message.'

Imogen forced herself back under control as she pushed down the kind of silly emotion and ideals about becoming engaged she'd always nurtured. They hadn't stopped it turning into a disaster last time with Gavin. The fact that he hadn't really wanted to get engaged, let alone married, that he'd been going along with what both sets of parents had thought was a done deal only made this moment all the more painful.

Marco had proposed—if you could even call it that—because she was pregnant. Gavin had just gone along with everyone's assumption they would one day get married. He hadn't loved her, and Marco most certainly didn't. At least this time she knew exactly where she stood. There would be no happy-ever-after and lifelong love from this ring either.

'It certainly does that.' She tried to be as detached as he was, tried to think of it as a deal she'd just struck instead of one of life's big events she seemed destined never to get right.

'Then that is the first part of our deal completed.' Marco signalled to the assistant to indicate that they had chosen the ring, and Imogen could only sit and watch in wonder as the transaction was completed. The deal was sealed. She was engaged. To a man whose child she carried, but, despite the large diamond on her finger, it was as far from the real thing as it could be.

She hung on to the fact that while this was just a deal it would at least enable her to make contact with her baby's grandparents, be able to tell her child in years to come about them. Those romantic notions made her smile, and then she thought of Marco, of the fact that, whatever else happened, as her baby's father he would be there in the background of her life for evermore.

That stark realisation was still ringing in her mind as she and Marco settled themselves in the back of his chauffeur-driven car a short while later. The weight of what the ring really represented was almost too much on her finger. 'What's next?'

'Now to the hospital.' He looked out of the window as he spoke and she wondered if he was more upset by his father's illness than he was letting on.

Compassion filled her heart and she wanted to reach out, place her hand on his arm, to reassure him that she was there for him. If she was in his position she would be distraught and so worried about her father. She didn't think she could be so outwardly calm and controlled about it. She slowly moved her hand towards him, wanting to help, to support him, the ring on her finger catching the light, sparkling brightly.

Marco took her hand, holding her fingertips in his, and looked from the ring to her. The atmosphere in the car so like it had been between them on the island. 'The ring sparkles almost as much as you, Imogen.' His voice was light and teasing. 'I hope that I can convince you to wear it always.'

'Will your father be feeling well enough for our visit?' she asked tentatively, trying to bring the conversation away from what the ring meant, what he really wanted from her.

'It would most likely cause him more stress to know you were here in New York and hadn't been to meet him.' Marco let her hand go. 'He cannot fail to like you, Imogen, and he and my mother are so excited they are finally to have a grandchild.'

'I hope you are right,' she said as she looked at him, his dark gaze holding hers, making her tummy flutter.

'He will appreciate the fact you have travelled

from England to meet him,' Marco said and something in his eyes softened. 'As I do.'

Imogen hadn't known how to respond to that and was thankful the car had arrived at the hospital. Now she swallowed down her nerves as they both stood on the threshold of the private hospital room Marco's father occupied. She'd never seen Marco look ill at ease and she glanced up at his profile as he took a deep breath and opened the door.

She followed him into the room and watched as he greeted his father in Italian and then sat down. He didn't give his father a hug, or kiss; there wasn't even a gentle, reassuring touch. She frowned as she watched his father look at Marco with sadness. Was Marco really that devoid of emotion he couldn't put aside whatever it was between them at a time like this?

Imogen felt awkward, as if she was intruding on something. This man and woman might well be her child's grandparents, but they were Marco's parents, his family. Marco took her hand, bringing her closer to him, pushing away all those questions just by being so close. 'Imogen, this is my mother, Mirella, and my father, Emilio.'

'So pleased to meet you,' his mother said quickly and stepped towards her and hugged her, so that she had to let go of Marco's hand. As his mother pulled away Imogen felt strangely adrift and looked at Marco, but he and his father were locked in what looked like eye combat, each glaring at the other. His mother must have seen her watching them, must have guessed she'd sensed the atmosphere, and spoke quietly. 'Two stubborn men.'

'So, you are to be a father,' Marco's father said firmly, his gaze not wavering from Marco's at all. Any chance of talking with Mirella now gone as the tension in the room seemed to rocket up, Imogen had no idea what was going on and looked from Marco to his father.

'We are both so excited. A new baby in the family.' Thankfully Mirella stepped in.

'It would be pleasing if the baby were a boy,' Emilio said, and when his attention flickered from Marco to her she'd never felt so in the spotlight before.

Imogen swallowed, not knowing what to say, wishing Marco would do something, say something, but all he seemed to want to do was continue the silent but angry animosity between him and his father.

'The son you never had?' Marco's words snapped across the room and Imogen looked from father to son, confusion mixing with the powerful tension which filled the room.

'Please, don't,' Mirella interjected, dragging Imogen's thoughts from what Marco had just said. She looked at him, but he turned from her, pointedly ignoring his father, and strode away from the bed. Imogen took in the firm set of Marco's shoulders and tried to make sense of what he'd just said, feeling more uncomfortable by the minute. What did Marco mean?

She looked again at Emilio and he put out his hand towards her, gesturing her close. She hesitated briefly then did as he asked, acutely aware of the increasing tension in the room. She had no idea what it was that had made Marco so angry, so hostile to his father, but whatever it was Marco had to fix it. If the unthinkable happened he might regret it for evermore.

The old man took her hand, focusing her mind, but not halting the whirl of questions. He spoke firmly but softly, his eyes sharp, his grip on her hand far stronger than she would have expected for a man so ill. 'Look after him.'

'The baby?' After the conversation that had just played out between father and son, Imogen wasn't sure who he was referring to.

'Marco. He is my son, no matter how he came into my life. He is my son.' Emilio closed his eyes for a second then opened them and looked at her, the darkness of his so like Marco's.

She frowned. 'I don't understand.' Her total confusion as to what was happening made the words come out in a rush when perhaps she should just have played along with it, pacified the old man.

He patted her hand with his free one and looked intently up at her. 'Just promise me you will look after him.'

Imogen nodded, wanting to offer some sort of hope to this man, but she had no idea what was going on, no idea what she was promising, but as he became agitated all she wanted was to smooth the moment over. 'I will look after him, yes.'

She didn't say anything more because that would be giving false promises. The lie she was already telling this sick old man by making him believe they were going to be married made it hard to say anything else.

She heard movement in the room and then felt the warm strength of Marco behind her. Did he also find it so uncomfortable to tell lies? Despite all he'd said, she wasn't convinced a baby was what Marco really wanted. So many thoughts whirled in her mind and when Marco placed his hand on her shoulder, bringing her close against him, the confusion deepened. The only clear thing in her mind was that there was so much anger between the two men; why did Marco feel the need to do this?

'We will see you at the party tonight, Mother.' Marco was aware his words were sharp as he kept his arm around Imogen, but he was desperate to bring the conversation back to something other than him and his father. Annoyance surged through him as he thought of what the old man had just said to Imogen, making him look the fool, the one who had grudges. If Emilio really felt that way he should have said it a long time ago instead of pushing him out, always making him feel different, not part of the family. He shouldn't have punished him all these years.

Marco vowed there and then that his child would never feel that isolation, that rejection. He wanted to be there, all the time, for his child, but convincing Imogen was another matter entirely. Imogen had not hesitated to tell him it was love she wanted. The one thing that had been in short supply throughout his childhood and the only emotion he didn't want to become embroiled in as an adult. The only emotion he couldn't give.

'Come and see me again, Imogen,' his father said, his voice frailer now after the exertion of the last few minutes. As he and Imogen made their way to the door, he felt her hesitation, saw the look of question she cast his way, and he knew what she was thinking. He could see it in her expressive eyes. She was already convinced that he was the hard and cold one.

'I'll come and tell you all about the party.' He didn't dare look at Imogen as she answered his father, but he could hear the smile in her words and from the satisfied expression on his father's face he knew she'd just played right into his hands.

He had no alternative but to explain to Imogen that the man lying in the hospital bed was not his natural father. It shocked him to realise that it mattered what she thought of him, something that had never featured in any of his previous affairs. But Imogen wasn't just an affair. She was the mother of his child.

It took him straight back to the conversation of moments ago, when he'd listened to his father's claim that he was his son no matter what. Anger had boiled through him, so powerful it threatened to blow like a geyser. Thankfully he'd contained it, focusing his thoughts instead on the knowledge that he couldn't ever turn his back on his child and that meant being part of its life—every single day. Whatever happened between him and Imogen now, he had to make her realise that the more permanent solution of marriage was the only way and that he intended to be in his child's life, to raise him or her as a Silviano.

'My sister will give my father a good account of the engagement party. There is no need to trouble yourself with visiting him again.' Marco snapped the words out at they sat in the car, moving slowly through the New York traffic towards his apartment. Imogen had remained silent as they'd left the hospital and he knew she'd sensed the tension between him and his father. He also knew she was full of questions. He could feel them every time she looked at him.

'It's no trouble,' she said lightly, looking out of the windows at the sights of the city as he turned to her. She must be so shocked by the rift between father and son that she couldn't now look at him. 'It's what you brought me here for after all.'

'There is no need.' Marco wasn't in the mood for this right now. All the times he'd been pushed aside as a child were now filling his mind.

'He is my baby's grandfather *and* he is ill,' Imogen said as she looked directly at him and he knew her questions were close to the surface. The light and breezy tone of her voice reminded him of blossom on a spring day, but he knew she was making a point. She was letting him know that she valued family and just what she thought of him for not doing so. 'But exactly what did he mean when he said you are his son, no matter what?'

'There are things about my father you don't know, things I didn't know until recently.'

Marco's mind raced back to the night when his father had first been admitted to hospital. His sister had gone home, leaving him with his father and mother, who'd sat beside the bed watching him sleep, and slowly the secret she'd kept for so long had come out.

He could still hear her say those words now: 'Your father's brother, the man you know of as the uncle who was killed in a traffic accident, is your natural father.'

He'd stood shocked beside the bed of his heavily sedated father, all hooked up to machines, and tried to take in all his mother had just said. For the first time in his life he'd been lost for words, but his mother hadn't finished.

'I'm not proud of it, but I had an affair, whilst Emilio and I were engaged. That affair resulted in you, and the rift it caused in the family was huge. But after the accident the man I'd first fallen in love with, the steady and sensible man lying there now—' she'd pointed to her husband ' —told me he still wanted to marry me, that it didn't matter who had fathered my baby.'

'Because I was the next Silviano generation?'

'Because he loved me,' she said softly, her expression begging him for forgiveness. 'And because he wanted to love you too.'

The realisation that his uncle had stepped into the role of father had left Marco numb and he hadn't been able to stay in the room with his mother or the man he'd always thought of as his father. Instead he'd fled to the small café his grandfather had started all those years ago, seeking the solace the old brick building always gave him. His mind had raced and all the missing pieces of his life, pieces he'd never realised were adrift, had slipped into place. No wonder he could never please his father. Despite what his mother had said, he'd resented him for being the son of his brother and when he didn't have a son of his own he'd punished him for being the next Silviano heir.

It had been then he'd known he had to get away from New York. Far away. His latest island acquisition had seemed the perfect place and, as he'd looked up at the old photo of his grandfather at the café, he'd felt as if he was being guided there by him. He never took time out to relax, but a covert visit to his newest resort would be close enough to escaping from the harsh reality of life for a while.

Mentally he shook himself and dragged his mind back to the present. All these revelations were making him fanciful. It was probably why he'd spent such a long time courting Imogen whilst they were on the island. The revelations of the past had got in the way of who he'd become and that was one thing he could never allow to happen.

'Things about your father? What sort of things?' Imogen spoke quickly, bringing him back from the past and shocking him with the intensity of her words. 'You brought me here, to parade me and my pregnancy to your father, and now you tell me not to see him again. What is going on, Marco?'

Shame tore through him. That was exactly what he'd done—at least, that was what he'd led her to believe, hardly able to believe himself that those feelings he'd had on the island were still there. He pushed them away, buried them with the pain of just who he really was, convinced they'd make him weak, and he looked at Imogen, willing her to understand, not to judge him.

Imogen finally gave in to the temptation to touch Marco and reached out to place her hand on his arm, feeling the muscles of his forearm flex and tighten as she did so.

'I'd be a fool not to notice that you and your father don't get on, that somehow you are trying to prove something by bringing me here to meet him.' She watched his profile turn sterner as she spoke and wondered if she'd gone too far. 'I want to see him again,

Marco. Family means everything to me and, whatever happens between us in the future, your parents are my baby's family.'

'I understand that, Imogen, but please don't think our baby is going to make the issues my father and I have better, because it won't.'

'How can you be so sure?' Her overwrought emotions threatened to get the better of her once more.

Marco gentled his tone, placed a hand over hers as it rested on his arm and looked at her, searching her eyes, and for a moment it was like being back on the island with her. But then her shutters rushed back up. 'The lie he and I have lived with has gone on too long to be undone.'

'But he's family.'

'Family, yes, but not my father. He made my mother keep it from me all these years, even had his name put on my birth certificate.' There was raw pain in Marco's voice now and her heart went out to him as she fought the need to hold him, to try and soothe his pain in the best way she knew.

'Why would he do that?'

'My mother had an affair with Emilio's brother, Giancarlo, whilst engaged to Emilio. They were found out, but just days later Giancarlo was killed in a car crash. My mother was pregnant—with me.'

'Oh, my goodness. Your father, or rather the man you've always thought of as your father, must really have loved your mother.'

'Maybe that's what it was.' The harshness of Marco's statement sent a shiver down her spine. 'But Emilio isn't my father.'

'Oh, Marco,' Imogen said softly, feeling his pain,

his confusion. 'The man lying in hospital is your father. He raised you. He even said you were his son.'

The car pulled up in front of a clothes store and Imogen inwardly groaned as the moment between them was snatched away. She'd almost found the real Marco.

Marco pulled his hand from hers, severed the connection which had nearly been made. 'I tried all my life to please him. Took his New York hotel chain and made it global, but it wasn't enough. I was always the disappointment, the son who didn't quite match up, and now I know why. I wasn't his son at all. I was his brother's child, and it wouldn't be his own son that would carry the Silviano name into the next generation.'

'You can't really believe that?'

He inhaled deeply, and she waited, but when he looked at his watch she knew the moment was gone. The openness lost. 'We have a few hours. I'm sure you will find something suitable here.'

Imogen didn't want to go in and buy anything. She wanted the car to continue driving around so that she could talk more with Marco, but from the firm set of his jaw she knew the conversation was over. He'd told her enough for her to understand why there was animosity between him and the man in the hospital, his father. Now it was clear there would be nothing more from him and, whilst she felt his pain, his sense of rejection, she couldn't understand why he'd ever thought that marriage was the solution.

'I'm not sure we should be doing this.' She ventured her opinion.

'What?' He frowned at her as he got out of the car and waited for her to do the same. 'Buy a dress?'

She almost laughed at his subtle humour, which reminded her of the man she'd met on the island, but reality quickly overruled that need. 'Go to the party, get engaged and yes, even buy a dress.'

He smiled at her retaliation. 'We need to do all of those things, Imogen. As I said before, I don't want anyone to question that we are engaged.'

'Why?' she asked as she walked through the doors of the store, her eyes widening when she saw the array of clothing on offer. It also niggled that he seemed comfortable in here with her and she wondered how many other women he'd kitted out for a party.

'Because I haven't yet given up on us getting married.'

'That isn't what I agreed to, Marco. I'm here just to meet your father—because he's ill.'

He paused as assistants hovered close by, but he didn't seem to notice them. 'We are having a baby, Imogen. We will be linked together through that child for ever, a child I want to bring up as a Silviano, so why not get married?'

'Because we don't love one another.'

He stared at her for a moment, then inhaled deeply. 'As I said, I haven't given up yet.'

Imogen was left stunned as he walked away towards the far side of the store. Did he really think everything would fall neatly into place just because he wanted it to? She looked at the assistants, wishing she and Marco were anywhere else but here. This needed to be sorted now.

He turned and looked at her, oblivious to her discomfort. Instead he gestured to the array of expensive dresses around her. 'This is my sister Bianca's favourite store, so I am positive you will find something for this evening.'

Moments later, Imogen was being whisked away to the dressing rooms by a very enthusiastic assistant. She tried various styles and various colours, all the time worrying what Marco was doing whilst she was in there. Finally, she stepped into a gold silk dress which had soft folds to help cover the bump of her baby.

'This is the dress,' she told the assistant, and went to show Marco.

His gaze travelled down her body so slowly she was sure she could feel his touch, but when he looked at her she saw the darkening of his eyes, and the suggestive hint of desire in them. It was how he'd looked at her the night she'd made love with him and a tremor of pleasure hurtled down her spine.

'*Bellissima,*' he said slowly, his seductive tone making desire unfurl within her. She should resist it, should fight it with all her strength, because if she didn't she was in danger of being the woman who'd longed for more than a one-week romance. If she stood any chance of walking away from him once the agreed two weeks were up, then she must not become *just* Imogen again.

'I think this one,' she stated boldly, trying hard not to allow her reaction to him show.

He nodded. '*Si*, that is the dress. Tonight you will dazzle New York.'

CHAPTER SEVEN

IMOGEN ENTERED THE party on Marco's arm, aware of everyone's scrutiny. The gold dress she'd finally settled on made her feel really special, although it didn't quite fully conceal the bump of their baby. She glanced around as they walked across the already crowded room and she could guess what some people may be saying about her and the baby, about why Marco had become engaged.

It made her nervous. Not that she'd ever show it. She held her head up, smiled at the guests who greeted them and kept close to Marco. It was one of the most uncomfortable things she'd done so far as part of the charade. The other had been telling her parents about Marco. Making them believe she and Marco were happy and in love had been as hard as having most of New York's elite society scrutinising her.

The discomfort wasn't helped by her annoyance and frustration that Marco had told her something of himself then shut the barriers and locked her out once more. As if to compensate for this he'd turned up the charm to lethal levels and already she could feel herself drawn to him once more, just as she had been on the island.

The ballroom of the imposing Fifth Avenue hotel was stunning and being here amidst all these people was like stepping out of reality all over again and into the world of escape she'd occupied on the island. Marco was attentive and looked so handsome in his tuxedo, and she knew that if she wasn't careful she'd succumb very easily to his charm, to the romance of the moment. It was luring her once more ever closer.

'So many guests!' she exclaimed as she held Marco's hand, not willing to let it go now despite her reservations about getting close to him again.

'My sister,' Marco said as he guided her towards two tall, slender, dark-haired women, 'Bianca.'

'I've heard so much about you,' Bianca said as she kissed Imogen on first one cheek then the other. Her warm smile was reflected in her eyes and Imogen liked her instantly. 'No wonder my brother wouldn't come back from his island retreat.'

Imogen laughed to cover the shock. Bianca knew about her and her time with Marco on the island? Did that mean he'd talked about her to Bianca before they'd met again in Oxford? A little gleam of hope began to swirl through her.

'And we are all so excited about the baby.' Bianca spoke more softly as Marco started chatting to other guests. 'A baby is just what Marco needs.'

There it was again. Marco *needed* the baby. 'It must have come as a shock,' Imogen said as Bianca's excitement trickled through her, pushing to one side that niggling doubt. She was sure she could talk to Bianca. Just maybe not right now.

'Not a shock, no. He's always known he would be the one to continue the family name,' Bianca said with a smile that briefly held sadness. 'It was a lovely surprise and I'm so happy you are getting married and staying in New York.'

'I'm not sure we've decided yet.' Imogen hoped this conversation wouldn't go deeper, wouldn't delve too much into the marriage she was slowly being backed into.

'Whatever you decide, I'm excited to have a new sister,' Bianca enthused as her attention was taken by more guests arriving. 'We'll talk again soon, but right now you and Marco have more guests to greet.'

As if on cue, Marco returned to her side, smiling down at her in a way that made a rush of something more than just desire-laden need course through her. She wanted this all to be real, but more than anything else she wished he *wanted* her and the baby as much as he *needed* them.

'Bianca is really nice,' Imogen said, trying to force her mind from things that couldn't ever really be.

'You say that as if I could never have a nice sister,' he joked with her as he took her arm and moved them towards a large gathering of men resplendent in tuxedos and women looking very elegant in cocktail dresses or long evening gowns. The whole thing was surreal. Never in her wildest dreams had she ever expected to be moving in such affluent and completely glamorous circles.

'I did wonder what she'd be like,' she teased as she smiled up at him. 'But she is not like you at all.'

His brows rose in mock indignation. 'Be careful, Imogen; if you tease me too much I might make you pay for that comment.' The dark look in his eyes sent warm shivers through her.

'Just how do you intend to do that?' She couldn't stop, the new light and carefree way they were right now so much like their time on the island. It was like having back the Marco she'd first met. The unguarded and very sexy Marco.

He moved a little closer to her, whispering seductively in her ear, 'I will kiss you until you can't do anything else but beg me for more.'

She blushed at the thought and her heart skipped a beat. This was the Marco she'd first met, and she wished she were alone with him right now, wished that he would do just that. Fortunately, she was saved from having to reply as an older man and his wife came to congratulate them, swiftly followed by more people until she was completely confused as to who was who.

The next few hours continued in the same way and Imogen tried not to feel anxious as the party atmosphere increased. So many people wanted to congratulate them that she was left in no doubt that Marco was held in high esteem by many people. It was only as the music slowed that she saw her first opportunity to talk to Marco about what Bianca had said.

'I think we should take to the floor now.' He smiled that charming and captivating smile he'd used whilst they'd been on the island, and she couldn't help but smile back. 'Everyone will be expecting us to dance.'

'I'd like that,' she said softly as memories of another night she'd danced with him rushed back. She placed her hand in his and followed him into the middle of the other dancers, the magic of the moment, the romance of the music seeping into her, threatening to dismantle the barriers she'd put up to protect herself from falling for this man.

The look in his eyes as he turned to her, took her in his arms, left her in no doubt he was fighting the attraction too. It was just like being on the island all over again. His palm was warm against her back as he held her. She moved towards him, unable to resist the urge to feel his body against hers again, and his brows rose as the bump of their baby pressed against him. His eyes darkened as he held her even closer.

The sensation shocked her. It was so intimate, so powerful, that it brought all the memories of their night together rushing back.

'We can't fight it for ever, Imogen,' Marco whispered in her ear, his breath sending stars of hot pleasure shooting all over her.

'We can.' Her whisper became husky as he held her tight against him, the bump of their baby between them, as if he was using it to remind her of what they'd had on the island. The night they had created this new life. 'It's not about us any more.'

'That's where you are wrong, *mia bella*.' His voice was so husky, so sexy, and dancing with him like this, when he was wearing his tuxedo as he had that last night on the island, was too much. It was testing her restraint, her ability to think rationally. She couldn't let him do this to her, couldn't allow herself to be carried away with the romance of the moment, not when she was only here with him because of the baby she carried. 'It is all about us. You, me and our baby.'

'Please, Marco,' she breathed the words, her heart thumping as it tried to rule her head, tried to make her believe what he was saying was real, 'don't say what you don't mean.'

He lowered his head, his lips so close to hers that at any second they might touch. 'I mean it, Imogen. Maybe this will prove it.'

He brushed his lips over hers so lightly it was like snowflakes landing on them in the winter, but the heat of his light and teasing kiss induced heat as hot as the desert sun. She shuddered in a deep breath, determined to resist him, determined to stop her heart getting carried away. A kiss didn't mean he could give her what she really wanted—love.

But a kiss did prove she was far from indifferent to him, that she still wanted him and the illusion of the fantasy they'd shared on the island. Was it so wrong to want one more night with him? Was it so wrong to indulge in the romance of the night one last time?

Whatever happened between them after tonight and no matter where they were in the world, they would always be tied to one another with the baby she carried. Surely, she could indulge in the fantasy a little more before returning to England?

Marco felt the warmth of Imogen's breath, tasted the sweetness of the orange juice she'd been sipping during the evening, but most of all he felt their baby between them. It jolted him, convincing him that keeping Imogen in his life, making her his wife, was not only what he needed, but what he wanted. There was no way he would allow his child to grow up without him in his life and, even though his natural father hadn't intended that to happen to his child, it had.

'That just proves we still want each other.' She

looked boldly at him. 'It doesn't mean we are meant to be together, Marco.'

She looked up at him, reproach in her eyes, and he had to stifle the urge to laugh—or kiss her. She looked so beautiful tonight, the gold dress showing off her glorious figure and her baby bump, and as he'd watched her talk with other people he'd been shocked by the swell of pride he'd felt. He'd tried to quell that pride, aware it was weakening him, putting him at the mercy of the kind of emotions he'd always shut out of his life. Now he looked down at her, wanting to banish those sentimental images she could so easily evoke. Imogen was his fiancée and carrying their baby—a baby that could be the son he needed. This woman was everything he needed. And more.

He had to convince Imogen that marriage, for so many reasons, was the right thing to do. 'We might well have escaped reality together whilst we were on the island, but that escape has crept into reality, Imogen, and now that reality has to change.'

'Please don't spoil tonight.' Her whispered plea was heartfelt and it made him feel something deep down, a kind of emotion he'd never felt before. 'Don't talk of tomorrow or any other day afterwards. I just want tonight to be about us, not reality.'

The message in her eyes was as clear as it had been that day on the beach as he'd revealed the surprise he'd created for their night of pleasure. She'd wanted him then, wanted so much more than just a kiss, and now that same desire shone from her eyes.

'Just tonight.' He whispered the promise against her lips as the music slowed to a stop.

She moved to lay her head on his shoulder and a

wave of protectiveness crashed over him. As the next slow song began he wrapped his arms around her more tightly, wishing they were alone in his apartment instead of here at the flagship hotel of Silviano Leisure Group.

'Can we leave now?' She lifted her head and looked up at him and the potency of the attraction between them sent a surge of hot need racing through him. If he didn't leave now he was in danger of losing his legendary control.

'*Si, mia bella.*' He hardly ever spoke Italian outside his family, but Imogen was unleashing something within him and Marco feared she was bringing down the barriers he'd long ago built, barriers he wasn't sure he wanted down. 'We can leave.'

He took her hand and wound his way through the throng of guests, wanting only one thing: to have Imogen to himself.

'Your mother has just arrived.' Imogen's words brought him to a halt and he couldn't help but tighten his hold on her hand.

Mirella had dressed for the party, so surely everything must be okay with his father, but still stinging panic shot through him. As he watched his mother survey the room, looking for either him or Bianca, he was aware of Imogen pressing against him, her free hand touching his arm.

'We should go to her.'

He nodded and sighed. 'Yes, we should.' Then he led Imogen over to his mother and watched her face light up in happiness as she saw them heading towards her. Guilt hit him like a rock hurled from close range. His mother believed things between him and

Imogen were real, and that belief made her happier than he'd seen her look for a long time. The stress of Emilio's illness had taken its toll on the once vibrant woman.

'There you are.' Her smile brightened further, intensifying Marco's guilt. He knew deep down that all his mother wanted was for him to be happy and settled in life. He was angry at the man she'd married, angry that he'd kept him at a distance all these years. At least now things made more sense. He just wished he knew why it had taken so long to tell him. Did his mother know how much she'd pushed her son away from the man she'd married?

'How is your husband?' Imogen asked as she felt the air prickle with tension. Marco's face had hardened with what she could only assume was annoyance and she wondered how the revelation of his parentage was really affecting him.

'He's quite well, thank you,' his mother said and turned her attention to Marco. 'Your arrival has certainly helped, and this little one—' she looked down at Imogen's tummy with pure affection before continuing '—this little one will bring the family together.'

Awkwardness filled Imogen. How did she respond to that, knowing all she did now about the revelation Mirella had only recently made to Marco?

'If the baby is a boy it will be the next Silviano heir no matter who my father is.' Marco's words snapped out. 'I have no secrets from Imogen. She knows the truth.'

Imogen sucked in a breath as hurt rushed across the older woman's face. She had no idea why she'd kept Marco's natural father a secret for so long, but she must have had good reason.

'He will indeed.' His mother focused her attention on Marco. 'But that isn't what matters to us, Marco. We are just happy you have found love.'

Marco frowned but his mother continued, 'Please don't blame Emilio any longer. Your father has been very sick and who knows how long this reprieve will last?'

Marco pushed his fingers through his hair and glanced down at Imogen, his gaze locking on hers, and for a moment it was only the two of them. The chatter of the guests, the music, everything, even his mother's presence, melted away. That powerful connection they'd shared on the island was there and in her eyes he could see her asking him to escape with her.

'Please try, Marco.' His mother's words seemed to jolt Imogen back to the party, back to the tension between mother and son.

Marco glanced at his mother then down at Imogen, smiling and feeling the tension leaving his face. 'I will; for Imogen and the baby, I will.'

His promise only embroiled Imogen deeper into the deception, and his guilt increased as he saw how uncomfortable she felt as his mother addressed her. 'Come and see us at the hospital again.'

'Yes, okay…'

'We will be at the hospital for a scan tomorrow. We'll call afterwards,' Marco interjected, and Imogen looked up at him. She'd smiled at his mother, played along with all he'd asked her to do, but those moments when she looked at him as she had done on the island made him feel that he was worthy of affection—maybe even love.

Imogen said goodbye to his mother as the reality of all he was asking of her charged through him. Annoyed at the direction of his thoughts, Marco strode out of the ballroom, not slowing his step, wanting to get away from the deception he now forced on Imogen.

'Slow down, Marco. I have heels on.' Imogen's voice held a note of panic and he stopped.

He turned to her, his guilt intensifying. 'I'm sorry, that was thoughtless of me.'

'It's okay,' she said as she reached out to him, and all he wanted to do was hold her, show her that the attraction which had brought them together was still there, despite the reality they were now in.

'Imogen,' he said huskily as he drew her to him, his palms sliding down her back, sparking off the passion which had been simmering beneath the surface all evening, 'I want you. I want to lose myself in the passion between us.'

He lowered his head and pressed his lips against hers, wanting so much more than just a kiss. Her body trembled as she clung to him. The idea of loving and being loved scared him. *Passion was what he needed*, he thought as her lips moved beneath his, coaxing that passion higher, her body begging his as it had done on the island. He wasn't afraid to give her *that*. He wasn't afraid to allow the passion to burn between them once more.

She moulded closer to him as his hands moved to her waist, then upwards in a trail of exciting exploration. Beneath his fingers, her nipple hardened, and she sighed into his mouth. He deepened the kiss as their desire rose.

A man coughing as he passed by made her pull away from him. She looked up at him, her blue eyes now dark with the same need which fired in him. 'Take me home, Marco,' she whispered as she snuggled against him.

'Nothing would give me greater pleasure.' He took off his jacket and put it around her shoulders.

He put his arm around her and walked towards the elevator, and just like that night on the island the passion which had just erupted between them once more had only one conclusion.

CHAPTER EIGHT

THE SLOWLY BUILDING desire between them was gaining in strength as Marco and Imogen entered his apartment. The ride home in the back of his car had been a test of his control he didn't want to have to endure again. The lights of New York had danced around the interior of the car, lighting Imogen's lovely face, showing her apprehension and making her look far too innocent. It had been this that had stopped him from continuing with what they'd started in the hotel right there in the back of the car. Now the elevator took them to his apartment and the need for restraint on the desire which thudded around his body was almost over.

Marco opened the door and stood back to watch as Imogen crossed the living area and went to stand at the windows, taking in the night-time view of New York which was wrapped seductively around them. He shut the door and stood there, watching her. She was seducing him, and she didn't even know it. Or was it that he was losing that vice-like grip on self-control? Not a comfortable thought and he focused his attention beyond the sexy image she created, trying to take in the view. It was as if he was seeing it for the first time—or maybe seeing it through Imogen's eyes.

'I'd like to go there,' she said absently, as if she wasn't even aware she'd spoken.

He moved a little closer, enjoying just watching her. The beautiful blonde looking over the sparkling lights of the city he'd always known as home. 'Where?'

'The Empire State Building.'

Marco fought with an onslaught of emotions as he turned his attention back to Imogen. He'd never taken women on dates like that, never pandered to their wishes, for fear of making them think there would be hope of a meaningful relationship. He'd always thought it safer to keep himself and his emotions locked away. But something had changed. He didn't want to be like that, be that hard and cold man, with Imogen. He wanted to make her happy. 'Then I shall take you there.'

He didn't look away from her, the iconic building forgotten as he took in the way the gold silk of her dress clung to her body. She looked so very sexy, and from the back he would never know she was carrying their child. He moved closer to her and stood right behind her, lowering his head to press a trail of kisses along her bare neck.

'Marco.' She whispered his name, sending the flames of desire within him leaping higher. His name had never sounded so sexy and he'd never wanted a woman so badly. She leant her head back against him and looked up, her lips parted as if begging him for more kisses.

He resisted the temptation and instead kissed along

her shoulder, bare apart from the thin strap of gold
silk. He traced his fingers down the same line he'd
kissed, but when they met the strap he slid it slowly
from her shoulder and then focused his kisses on the
other shoulder. Again, he slid the strap down. He
wanted the soft gold silk gone from her body, wanted
to slowly pull down the zip at the back of the dress.

'I want you, Imogen.' He breathed the words over
her skin, flames of desire licking ever higher around
him. 'Tonight.'

He'd do anything to feel that freedom he'd found
the night he'd spent with Imogen on the island. It
had been like no other affair he'd had, and he wanted
to experience exactly that feeling all over again. He
drew in a sharp breath, calling on his strength of
control. He didn't want to push her too far, too soon.

Her breath shuddered from her. 'I want that too,
Marco.' He knew she was answering his statement,
but he was sure she was agreeing to his thoughts.

His fingers touched the bare skin of her back as he
took hold of the zip and began sliding it downwards,
exposing the soft, creamy skin of her back. Unable
to resist, he lowered his head and pressed his lips at
the top of her spine, kissing lower and lower as he
pulled down the zip.

Imogen gasped as she clutched the gold fabric to
her breasts, but the arching of her spine left him in
no doubt she didn't want him to stop. Just as she had
been that night on the island, she was as driven by
desire as he was.

She turned round slowly. 'Do you always seduce
women in your window for all to see?'

'Never.' He shook his head as the image of her

burnt into his mind, into his soul. Erotically wild needs rushed through him and all he could think about was seeing her naked, seeing every bit of her, seeing the swell of their child in her belly. 'Let the dress go, Imogen. It's just us and the night sky up here.'

A teasing smile played at the corners of her mouth and the Imogen he'd brought to New York gave way to the sexy Imogen he'd made love to on his island. 'Are you certain about that?'

'Absolutely,' he said as he stepped back to take in the sexy picture of her, hair tousled by his kisses, face flushed by desire, as her dress clung to her amazingly curvy body.

His pulse beat wildly in his head as her smile widened, became more provocative and sexy. 'In that case…' she teased.

She let the fabric slip from her grasp and it slithered like liquid gold to the floor, leaving her naked apart from the skimpiest panties he'd ever seen and sexy gold strappy heels. Her arms still covered her breasts, but their fullness couldn't be hidden completely as his gaze travelled down her body, over her breasts and to the soft swell of her tummy.

'Dio mio,' he said hoarsely, unable to move, unable to take his eyes from her as hot lust stabbed through him. If he touched her now there would be no stopping. *'Bellissima.'*

'I don't understand Italian,' she said softly as she walked towards him. 'But I do know what that means. Nobody has ever called me beautiful before.'

'Then I will say it again, Imogen. You are beautiful.' He stepped closer as he fought for control, taking her face between his hands, kissing her lips and trying valiantly to ignore the fact that she was virtually naked as he spoke against the fullness of her lips. 'So very beautiful.'

'If you say it again I might begin to believe you.' The laughter in her voice, the teasing edge to it, was in complete contrast to the woman who stood looking up at him, vulnerability in her eyes. He'd known vulnerability like that when he'd stood before his father as a young boy while the reprimands rained down. He'd been desperate for his father's love.

Did Imogen feel the same? Was she desperate for him to love her? He dragged the heated desire back to the fore, refusing to think about anything but taking Imogen to his bed once more. She moved towards him, calming his wild emotions, and he allowed the passion and desire to reign, quashing any need for thoughts.

'You are beautiful, Imogen.' He spoke softly, almost in a whisper, as his lips brushed over hers. The sentiment of the moment was getting to him, dragging him back to that place Imogen had taken him to on the island.

Imogen held her breath as Marco whispered those precious words against her lips. Her body trembled. She was almost naked. Marco's seductive look had made her bolder than ever, empowered her, sweeping away all the doubt over her curvier figure Gavin's betrayal had induced. The memory of Gavin's mocking words had made her far too self-conscious when she'd first met Marco, but now she could so easily fall under Marco's powerful spell. It would be all too easy to pretend this was more than just lust, to fall in love with him, and she was afraid that if she didn't hold on to her wayward emotions she would do just that.

'Marco.' She whispered his name quietly, allowing herself to dream, to believe they were back on the island, back in their moment of escape. If he did love her, would it be like this?

She drew in a breath as he laid his palm over her tummy, over the small bump of their baby. She looked at him, his head still lowered, his eyes downcast. Just as a shimmer of panic began to set in he looked at her, his dark eyes full of an emotion she couldn't fathom, the expression on his face like none he'd worn before. It was as if the reality of the baby was sinking in for the first time. She hoped that when they went for the ultrasound scan tomorrow he would be as overwhelmed by it all.

'My baby,' he whispered as he kept his hand over her tummy.

'Our baby,' she said as she looked at him, wishing they could stay in this moment for ever, that reality didn't have to return. 'And we will be able to see it tomorrow.'

'Yes,' he said as he pressed his lips to her tummy. 'But right now I have more important things to think of.'

She looked up at him warily, trying to maintain some dignity after her uncharacteristic boldness of moments ago. 'What things?'

'Taking you to my bed.' He kissed her softly, his arms wrapping around her, pulling her close, forcing her to stop shielding her breasts and wrap her arms around his neck. 'Taking us both somewhere we can escape once more. Lose ourselves in each other as if nothing else matters.'

It was what she wanted more than anything else, to be in his arms once more. She wanted him with a powerful need she'd never known before and if one more night of escape was all he was offering she would take it, hoping more would follow, hoping the baby she carried would be everything he needed and bring them together.

Emboldened by her need for him, Imogen forgot her state of undress, forgot everything but savouring this moment. 'Then take me to your bed, Marco. I want to escape with you.'

In one swift movement Marco swept her off her feet and carried her across the vast apartment with its masculine minimalist furnishings. At the door to his bedroom, a room she hadn't been in, he paused. 'I could be doing this for real if you agreed to my suggestion.'

'Doing what for real?' She laughed, wondering where the seriousness had suddenly sprung from.

'Carrying you over the threshold.'

'You do that when you get married.' She laughed again, but the expression in his eyes warned her he wasn't laughing.

'Which is what I think we should do.'

'Don't spoil it,' she whispered as the intensity in his eyes deepened. If he loved her, if he really wanted her, then she would marry him, but it wasn't love which brought them together now, it was lust. Not the foundation for marriage she wanted. 'I don't want to talk about this now.'

'I have ways of making you change your mind.'

The charm was back, the intensity diminished, as he laughed and opened the door. 'First I will kiss you all over.'

'Sounds delicious.' She giggled, shocking herself at the sound. 'Then what?'

'I will make passionate love to you all night. I'm going to prove to you that the fire of passion that burns between us, along with the baby you carry, means we should be married.'

Imogen's heart skipped a beat. He wanted to make *love* to her. Did that mean he felt something more than just sexual attraction for her? Hope flared brighter than any firework, bringing down the wall she'd built around her heart since Gavin had betrayed her trust, her love, so terribly.

'The fire of passion?' she repeated huskily as he stood by the bed, holding her so that she could feel the thud of his heartbeat. Was he trying to say that he could give her what she wanted?

He laid her on the bed and stood up to pull at his tuxedo jacket, discarding it by flinging it to the floor, hastily removing his tie and shirt. She watched as he leant over her, his biceps flexing as he kept his weight off her.

He began the same torment he'd unleashed that night on the island, kissing down her throat, down to her breasts, which ached for his touch. He then moved lower and pressed a gentle and lingering kiss to her tummy and she closed her eyes against the onslaught of emotions.

She lay with her eyes closed and felt the bed dip as he moved away. If she opened her eyes now it would be like going back to that moment on the beach, to the moment she'd tried to imagine that this was what it would be like to be loved by him. She'd fooled herself then with the fantasy of being with him and even though she knew it wasn't enough, that they couldn't build a marriage on that, she could so easily fool herself again tonight.

His touch when he took her ankle in his hand startled her. She opened her eyes and looked at him, watched that sexy smile spread slowly over his lips, and her heart filled with the kind of emotions she'd thought she'd never feel again. This time, though, it was different. Those fledgling emotions were far more powerful than anything she'd felt for Gavin.

'These need to come off,' he said seductively, dragging her mind from its foolish course of analysing her feelings. With care, he undid the straps of her gold sandals and dropped one to the floor, then did the same again, his fingers rubbing over her foot, up her ankle. He smiled at her and her heart flipped as the need to be really loved by him took over. She wished this were more, wished this moment were real, instead of the escape he'd already labelled it.

Just as he had done that night on the beach, he slid his palms up her legs and began the exquisite torture, but this time it was different, far more pleasurable than she'd ever believed possible, and all she could do was close her eyes as he expertly brought her almost to the edge. Just when she didn't think she could hold on any longer he ceased the torment, focusing instead on pulling the lace panties down her legs before tossing them to the floor. She watched in awe as he all but tore off his remaining clothes and then gently moved over her, covering her nakedness with his body.

She closed her eyes and lost herself in the moment, indulging in the fantasy of being loved by Marco one more time.

Marco resisted the urge to let go, to give in to his body's demands and lose the last remaining bit of restraint he had. He wanted to be gentle, wanted to make this as pleasurable for Imogen as it had been that first night they'd made love on the beach. He struggled to keep control as Imogen wrapped her legs around him. The hot lust that had drawn them together on the island was certainly still well alight and all he wanted to do now was to prove, not only to Imogen, but also to himself, that it would bring them closer, that this was what they needed to make a marriage work.

The passion drove him and as he slowly entered her he stopped thinking of anything other than the pleasure of the moment. Right now nothing else mattered, and as her body moved with his, taking them once more to the heights of pleasure they'd discovered on the beach, he could think of nothing else other than this woman, this moment.

'Marco, Marco…' She gasped his name as her fingers dug into his shoulders, her legs tight around him. He forced himself to be gentle, aware of her condition, but her seductive voice threatened his control as her body begged for release.

He kissed her, stopping himself from saying anything to her, stopping her from saying anything else to him. Words weren't needed to show her how right they were together. The passion and heat of the moment would prove that.

She gasped against his mouth as the tidal wave of passion swept her away, taking him with her. He used every last bit of control to keep his movements gentle, wanting the moment to go on, but finally his body was sated and he moved off her, pulling her close against him, breathing in the scent of her perfume as she wriggled her back against his tummy.

He placed his hand on her tummy, over the small but definite bump of the baby, and closed his eyes, never having known such peace, such contentment.

He must have slept, although he had no idea how long for. When he woke Imogen had slipped from the bed and, wearing his shirt, stood looking out at the same view his living area offered as the grey streaks just before dawn were starting to show in the sky.

He'd never fallen deeply asleep with a woman after having sex before. At least not the satisfying sleep he felt he'd just indulged in, and he'd never encouraged closeness with a woman in the way he had when he'd pulled Imogen against him. Was it just because she was carrying his child? The question lingered at the edges of his mind then he pushed it away, focusing again on Imogen looking at the view.

In a way he'd never known before, he wanted to please her to make her happy, and if that meant doing the tourist thing and going up the Empire State Building, he'd do it. 'I will take you there today.'

'Did I wake you?' Her voice was husky with the remnants of passion. Her lovely blonde hair was fluffy and so very sexy and his shirt skimmed the tops of her thighs. The image made him want her all over again.

'It's early. Come back to bed.' He pulled back the sheet, revealing his hardened body, smiling with satisfaction as her eyes were drawn to his erection. 'The night isn't over yet and I'm not through with proving how we could make our marriage work.'

'Last night was amazing.' She blushed as she moved back towards the bed, his shirt open, revealing her tummy and teasing him with glimpses of the softness of her breasts. 'But it isn't what keeps a marriage together, Marco.'

He hadn't been banking on such a serious discussion even before the heat of passion had cooled. Caught out by his naked and aroused body, he pulled the sheet back over himself and lay back on the pillow, his hands behind his head, his gaze still focused on the woman who carried his baby. He took in a deep breath and knew there would be no escaping this discussion.

'What about a baby, Imogen? That is a reason to keep a marriage together, is it not?'

'It is, yes.' He smiled at her answer. He was wearing her down, making her see that marriage was the only option for them. He wanted his child, the potential heir to the Silviano empire, to be born inside marriage.

'Good,' he said, satisfied it had been so easy. 'Then we will get married. Next month.'

'Next month?' Her soft laughter lightened the seriousness of his words. 'Why the hurry?'

'Our child is my heir. My mother is desperate that I marry and, now that she knows we have a baby on

the way, it will be expected that we will marry before the baby is born.' He couldn't tell her that if the
baby was a boy that he'd finally be proven a man in
Emilio's eyes.

'But I've told you that is not a reason to marry,
Marco.' Imogen dragged his mind back from the past,
sadness filling her words, and he sensed that talking
about this wasn't enough. He'd accept that for now
but knew he would have to show her how good her
life could be as his wife—and not just in his bed.

'Come back to bed and rest. We have a busy day
today. We'll see the sights of New York from the Empire State Building then go to the hospital for the scan
and afterwards see my father.'

'You will be with me when I have the scan?' she
asked as she curled up next to him and he smiled,
sensing she was giving in.

'I want to see the baby… and we can find out if it
is a boy or a girl.'

She turned in his arms and looked up at him, smiling. 'You really are taking this seriously, aren't you?'
The teasing edge to her voice was back and a pang of
guilt rushed through him.

'I am. I'm taking it very seriously.' He kissed her
as passion rose once more.

CHAPTER NINE

THE SUN WAS warm on Imogen's face as she and Marco stepped outside on floor eighty-six of the Empire State Building along with many tourists. He'd laughed gently at her shock that the elevator had gone up so fast, the floor numbers only showing in units of ten, and that laughter had only lulled her deeper into that false sense of security. It had made it easier to believe they were a proper couple who were in love and having a baby.

Everything about being with Marco since the party last night was overwhelming. She could feel herself falling for him in a way she'd never fallen for any other man before. She thought what she and Gavin had shared was love but now she was questioning that idea. The way she felt about Marco was far different. It deepened with each smile, each gentle touch. The tenderness of the way they'd made love this morning had been the moment she realised that it wasn't escape she sought in his arms, it was love.

'I have to take some pictures,' Imogen said as she pulled out her phone and moved to the corner of the building and looked out across the streets of New

York. 'If I don't send Julie at least one picture of New York she will be furious.'

Behind her she could feel Marco's presence, feel the warmth of his body as he stood so very close to her. Even with all the people around them it felt intimate and she couldn't help but lean to one side and look back up at him. The ever-darkening intensity of his eyes held her attention and for a moment it was just the two of them there. As if time had stood still and nobody else mattered. Just as she had last night and this morning, Imogen felt that connection with Marco that she'd had on the island.

He took the phone from her hand. 'In that case I will get someone to take a photo of us both here. I want Julie to see how happy you are, how your smile is making your eyes sparkle, how you look so alive and so very beautiful.'

She tried hard not to read more into his words, instead convincing herself that this was all part of his ploy to get what he wanted, to keep her in New York and for his baby to be born here. That was all he meant, and she'd be a fool to read more into it. A fool to even think of marrying him for anything other than love.

'That's not necessary. I just need a few view photos, then I will call her later today.' The last thing Imogen wanted was for Julie to see what Marco had just described. If she did see that there was no way she would support her decision to return to England and raise the baby alone. Imogen knew that even though her deepening feelings for Marco were clear for all to see, Julie already suspected as much if their earlier calls were anything to go by. Julie had heard it in her voice, claiming Imogen had fallen for him long before she herself had accepted this. Did his mother and father see it too? Had his sister seen it? The only person that didn't see it was Marco. He didn't want anything to do with love.

That sobering thought silenced her and before she could say anything Marco was asking the other couple to take a photo of them. She couldn't back out of it now without making a scene, so she leaned into Marco as he put his arm around her, pulling her close. She tried to keep the love she knew she now had for him from showing, tried to keep that secret light from her eyes. As the heat of his body warmed hers, she knew it was going to be a hopeless battle. She'd fallen in love with him.

'Smile,' instructed the man as his girlfriend watched on. They looked the perfect couple as they laughed together while he prepared to take the photo. They were a couple who were happy and in love. Everything Imogen wanted but couldn't allow herself to believe was possible for her and Marco.

Imogen forced herself to smile, acutely aware of Marco's body against hers. She glanced up at him, confusion rushing through her. Why was he indulging her in this fantasy, this illusion of their being a couple?

'Look this way,' the man called as other people waited for the photograph to be taken. She smiled, painfully aware that this might be the only photograph she'd have to show their child one day of her and Marco together as a couple.

The man gave the phone back to Marco, who showed her the photos that had been taken of them in one of New York's most iconic places. She was right to worry about Julie being ever more convinced that what she now felt for Marco was more than just attraction. It was there in her smile and in her eyes as they stood together in the photo. She could see it, and Julie most definitely would, but not Marco, or at least he didn't seem to want to see it. He was oblivious to that emotion.

'When I was in your office in Oxford and Julie walked out the door she gave me a warning look.' Marco spoke as he leant on the stonework and looked through the metalwork railing, appearing to see the city, but Imogen guessed his thoughts were far away.

'I know.' Imogen spoke softly as she moved closer to him, finding it easier to look out over the view than at the man who now held her heart. The reality was that Julie's warning that he shouldn't hurt her would inevitably come true. She'd fallen in love with a man who'd already claimed he didn't want love in his life.

'So the man you were engaged to hurt you?'

'He did, yes.'

'What happened? It must be bad for your friend to be so protective.'

'There's no need to talk about it now. That part of my life is over and done with.' Imogen moved slowly away from Marco and began to walk to the next side of the building, to a different view of New York. As she stood and looked out over the vastness of buildings, all shapes and sizes, she could feel his eyes on her, feel the questions he wanted to ask following her.

He came to stand beside her once more, his upper arm brushing against hers sending a jolt right through her. Even though she knew he wasn't right for her, even though she knew that there was no future for them together, she still wanted him.

'I'd like to know, Imogen. After all, you know a lot about me now.' She couldn't resist the temptation to look at him and turned to face him. There was genuine sincerity in his eyes, which only served to make her feel as though she was falling that bit more in love with him.

Imogen took a deep breath. 'Gavin and I grew up together and sort of fell into a relationship. It was what our families expected, and we'd been dating for almost eighteen months when he proposed.' It didn't feel right talking about her past like this with a man she knew could never love her, even though she'd fallen in love with him. The fact that she could now admit to herself she loved Marco was unnerving and she hated that it made her vulnerable. As if love itself was exposing her to hurt and pain she'd never known before.

'So what went wrong?' He seemed interested, concerned, but was he just making conversation, was he just ensuring he knew her secret past because she knew his? There was no way she would admit the whole truth and tell Marco how Gavin had finally admitted to asking her to marry him because his mother had all but forced him to.

'He broke it off just weeks before we were due to be married.' She shrugged away the hurt from that day. 'I guess he wasn't ready to commit after all.'

She could still hear Gavin's break-up speech now. She'd been trying on her wedding dress for the final time when he'd rung. 'We should have stayed friends. I just don't fancy you.'

She'd soon found out that another woman had made him change his mind. She was a woman as slender as Imogen was curvy and all her insecurities about her body, her weight, had charged back at her like a wild animal. It hadn't helped when she'd seen on social media that Gavin had married the other woman in a lavish ceremony in Spain. It had been that information, along with Julie's advice, which had pushed Imogen into the mindset of moving on as she'd flown to the island. It had also ultimately pushed her into Marco's arms.

She glanced at Marco's profile as he looked out over his home city and when he turned to her she spoke again quietly, embarrassed and humiliated by the fact it had happened to her. 'He married someone else earlier this year.'

Guilt rushed through Marco as he saw the pain and hurt on her face. She must have loved this Gavin. The fact that she couldn't quite look at him now, that she focused her attention back to a view he knew she didn't really see, left him in no doubt of that. Was trying to convince her to marry him the right thing to do? It seemed the odds were stacked against them. She wanted love and family, and since discovering he was to be a father all he wanted was his child. If the baby was a boy he would be able to prove once and for all that even in Emilio's strict parameters, he was worthy of the Silviano name.

Imogen placed a hand on her tummy, the movement catching his attention, reminding him that the reason they were here together like this, sharing secrets they'd rather not tell anyone, was because of the baby she carried. He'd been intrigued enough by the woman he'd met on the island to try and track her down but hadn't thought further than indulging in more passionate nights with her. He'd never expected to stumble across the real Imogen so easily and he'd certainly never anticipated being a father, being linked by a baby with the woman he'd affectionately remembered as *just* Imogen.

As he thought of the baby it reminded him of the appointment he'd made for this afternoon. It had been nineteen weeks since they'd been on the island together and he'd been informed by the clinic that the scan would be able to tell them the sex of the baby. He didn't want to ask Imogen to find out if she didn't want to know, but *he* really wanted to know. He needed his father to know that he would marry the woman who carried his child, that he too would put the needs of future generations of the Silviano family first, whatever the sex of the baby.

If nothing else, the truth of who his father really was had made Marco realise that having the son Emilio had always pressured him to have would prove he could do something right.

He brushed his palm against Imogen's cheek and she looked up at him, questions in her eyes. 'Gavin was a fool.' As he said those words another thought slipped in through his mind. Gavin's stupidity would be his gain, but he resisted the urge to say that to her, knowing it wasn't what she would want. She'd already told him the only thing she wanted from marriage was love. The very thing he wasn't worthy of—Emilio had taught him that when he'd showered love and affection on his sister, pushing Marco out. It had left him in no doubt that he didn't belong, didn't deserve love and affection.

'Everyone has things in their past that upset them.' She looked up at him and he saw anger in her eyes, mixing with the pain of her past. 'But it has to be put aside, not forgotten and maybe not even forgiven.'

He looked deep into her lovely eyes. He knew she wasn't referring to Gavin. 'You think I haven't done that?'

She lowered her lashes and shook her head, then looked back up at him as tears filled her eyes. 'No, Marco, you haven't.'

'Then I must try.' He saw the hope in her eyes and knew it was wasted on him. There was no way his past could be so easily mended. He couldn't brush over it as if it had never happened. Just as he couldn't have this conversation any longer.

He took her hand and led her to the side of the building with the view out towards Central Park in the distance. Around them other sightseers laughed and exclaimed over the views they saw but right now all he could focus on was Imogen.

He couldn't help himself any longer. He had to kiss her again and bring back the flames of desire to drown all she'd opened up. He had to taste her lips on his once more and he had to do it now. He lifted her chin and lowered his head to press his lips tenderly against hers. The light contact sparked the heated desire they'd shared last night once more. He caught her sigh as she breathed into the kiss, he felt her body mould to his as she wrapped her arms around him.

He'd never experienced anything like this before. For him dating women was all about glamorous parties, high-end meals, being seen in the right places before taking his date home and giving in to the primal urge of sex. It was as if this kiss actually meant something. Was it because she carried his baby? A child he would see in just a few hours when they attended the scan.

Excitement and trepidation rushed through Imogen as her baby's image came up on the ultrasound screen. She couldn't take her eyes from its movements, even when Marco leaned closer and took her hand, bringing him so very close to her. She focused her attention on the screen, on her baby, trying to ignore how close Marco was as well as the seemingly never-ending beeps as measurements of the baby were taken. Imogen panicked. Was this normal? Was her baby okay?

'Is the baby all right?' she asked anxiously, aware of Marco's gaze flying to her face then to the sonographer, who instantly reassured them that everything was perfectly normal, and Imogen relaxed. She looked up at Marco again, but his attention was now solely focused on the screen, where the image of their baby was moving, first an arm, then a leg. Imogen couldn't help but laugh softly at it. That was her baby.

'I can't believe it. Look, it's moving,' Marco said, his voice a husky whisper of wonder, and she looked up at him, saw the wonder on his face as he watched the limbs of his baby move. She studied his face, felt the smile playing on her lips, and knew it was too late for her. She loved this man. Her smile slipped. Would he ever love her?

'That's our baby,' Imogen said very softly as she held Marco's hand tighter, tried to convey without words how she felt about this moment, about him. As he looked down at her she could almost believe he was doing the same.

'There's the heartbeat.' The sonographer's voice caught their attention, breaking the spell, and they looked at the screen again.

'Oh, my goodness. I can see its heart beating,' Imogen said, her voice barely a whisper as all sorts of emotions rushed through her. Seeing her baby on the screen, seeing its heart beating, just made everything feel so much more real. Happiness flooded through her. She might not be in a proper relationship with her baby's father, but she was really happy about impending motherhood. She wanted to shower this baby with everything she possibly could, but most of all she wanted to give it love. Lots of love. She didn't want her child to ever doubt how much it was loved and wanted.

'Can you tell its sex?' Imogen's gaze flew to Marco as he spoke. It wasn't just the sudden harshness of the words after the emotion of moments ago, it was the question itself. Was it really that important for him to know?

Imogen reluctantly admitted that it was vital he know, and it wasn't just Marco who would be waiting for news. The whole reason she had been brought to New York, paraded as his fiancée and mother of his child, she now knew, was not to make his father happy but to prove a point. Whatever it was that had gone on between them in the past was still very much there. She could only guess what Marco needed to prove to his father and that guess was that he could produce the next Silviano boy. To do that he needed this baby to be a son. The sadness of the situation trickled through her like an icy cold mountain stream as she recalled his words in Oxford: *You have what I need.*

'Would you like to know?' the sonographer asked as she rolled the transducer over Imogen's tummy. A part of Imogen wanted to say no, then as she looked at the firm set of Marco's jaw she knew that they both needed to know, but for very different reasons.

'Yes, yes, please, I'd like to know.'

Imogen lay there and closed her eyes, not daring to look at the screen, and she felt Marco's fingers tighten around her hand. She could feel his tension and knew that not only her whole future hinged on this moment, but also that of her child's.

'There we are.' The sonographer paused her movements over Imogen's tummy and as the bleep sounded once more Imogen opened her eyes and looked at the screen. She had no idea what she was expecting to see but she couldn't tell whether the baby was a boy or girl and, judging by the ever-tightening grip on her hand, neither could Marco.

'Is it a boy?'

Imogen's heart thudded harder as Marco's question, full of aggressive hope, seemed to slice the tension in the room. If the sonographer was aware of it, she was doing a very good job of hiding her shock.

'It's a girl.'

'A girl?' The question rushed from Marco, the harshness in his tone something Imogen had never heard from him before, and right there and then her world crashed down around her.

Marco didn't want a girl. Marco needed a son. A Silviano heir to make a point to his father, to prove whatever it was he was so desperate to prove. Over the last day or so Imogen had allowed herself to hope, had allowed herself to believe that maybe whatever it was that was between her and Marco was enough to build a marriage on, for the baby's sake. Now, in just one split second, everything had changed.

'And is she healthy? Is everything as it should be?' Marco demanded, sounding more like he was in the boardroom than the hospital seeing the first glimpse of his baby.

'Yes, yes. Everything is just fine. Your little girl is just as she should be at nineteen weeks.'

'Good.' Marco stepped away from where Imogen lay, letting go of her hand, and she could feel herself drifting from him already, as if he was more than physically stepping back from her.

Imogen refused to allow him to spoil the moment. This was her baby, her little girl, and just because it wasn't what he wanted she was not going to allow him to darken this moment. She focused her attention firmly on the screen as a few final measurements were taken. She didn't want to look at Marco, she didn't want to see the disappointment in his face.

Feeling more as if she was in some kind of nightmare, Imogen sat up and sorted her clothing, all the time keeping her attention off Marco. She just couldn't look at him yet, couldn't face seeing the disappointment in his face. The tension in the room climbed ever higher. She had to get out; she couldn't stay in this confined space with him for much longer.

'I need some fresh air,' Imogen said as she forced back the emotions that were rushing at her like a tidal wave, making her head spin and bringing back the nausea.

'It's very hot today,' the sonographer sympathised as she turned to face Imogen. She looked at Marco. 'Perhaps your husband will take you outside for some air.'

It was on the tip of her tongue to say they weren't married, but the thought that would never now be true made her want to cry. He didn't *need* a daughter and he didn't need her. The fact that she had fallen in love with him was irrelevant. She fought harder to keep back the tears, determined not to show any kind of weakness. Not in front of Marco.

'We will get some air then go and see my father while we are at the hospital.' There was a definite crispness to his voice and the panic Imogen had felt the moment she knew their baby was a girl intensified further, making her head ache.

'Are you going to tell him? About the baby being a girl?' Tentatively she asked the question, taken aback when he looked at her, his eyes dark and forbidding.

'I have never pleased my father yet. I have spent all my life trying to and only recently I found out why I could never succeed.' He stopped, his hand reaching out to her, forcing her to look at him. His gaze held hers as they blocked the hospital corridor and she could see the shock, the disappointment in them. 'No, I am not going to tell him. He doesn't need to know.'

Those words were the death knell to any hope she had that she and Marco might really work. He was ashamed of his daughter, and in her eyes that meant only one thing: he would never be able to love her or his daughter and would never be able to be the kind of father she'd had. Family had been the most important thing in her life and despite the passion she and Marco had shared, despite the attraction still crackling between them, he could never be the family man she'd always dreamed of marrying.

'Perhaps you should tell him,' she broached gingerly, trying to protect herself, her heart, as much as anything. 'Maybe it would be better to be honest now.'

'I'll handle this my way.' The harshness of his tone cut her already battered emotions, but she refused to let him see the hurt.

She placed her hand on his arm. 'We can do this together.'

'Perhaps I should go alone.' Why did he always push her away?

'He is our daughter's grandfather.' It was a fact neither of them could escape and she watched Marco's jaw clench in annoyance at the truth of her words.

'As you wish,' he said as he began to walk along the corridor, leaving her no option but to follow as they made their way to his father's room on the other side of the hospital.

CHAPTER TEN

MARCO DID AS he always did when he spent any time in his father's company: he prepared for the feeling that he'd failed him and the Silviano name. He also knew that this time he'd failed Imogen—he'd let her down. He'd been so shocked when the sonographer had said the baby was a girl that all hope he could finally do something to gain his father's approval had evaporated. He shouldn't have let his shock show. He should have considered how Imogen would feel. He'd brought her to New York because of the baby she carried, because he wanted to prove to his father that he could and would step up to his responsibilities. He'd hoped for a son, one to inherit the family fortune after him. He'd never considered the implications if the baby was a girl.

As Imogen had looked at him he saw the closeness they'd found slipping away. He saw it in her eyes, in the way she'd moved as she stood up and adjusted her clothing. She hadn't been able to do it quick enough, as if she wanted to hide the baby from him. She was upset, hurting, and he'd done that to her. Driven on by a selfish need to prove himself, he'd hurt the one person who'd wanted to be with him because of who he really was, not who he always tried to be.

He opened the door to his father's private room and walked in before his nerve deserted him. Yet again he was going to have to be a big disappointment to the man who'd brought him up as his own son, keeping the Silviano family name going. This was exactly what he'd been escaping from when he'd gone to his island retreat: family drama.

'How lovely to see you both again.' His mother beamed as she got up and came to them, greeting Imogen with a kiss and hug. A pang of guilt snapped at him. He was going to be letting her down too. She'd been putting pressure on him for several years to marry, to give her grandchildren. He'd thought when his sister had done that last year the pressure would slacken. It hadn't. A boy, born to a Silviano son, was needed and it was his duty to provide that. He just couldn't decide if his mother's loyalties lay with his natural father, the lover she'd lost before she'd become a Silviano, or her husband, the man who'd taken on his brother's son. A son that would be the only one he had after his two daughters were born.

He pushed all the bad-tasting thoughts from his mind, not wanting to drag Imogen deeper into the complexities of his family life. As he walked towards the bed he looked at his father, pleased to see he seemed in better spirits than he had for a long time. 'You are looking better.'

'I will be even better when I get out of here,' his father snapped, but Marco didn't miss the wink of conspiracy he gave his mother. They looked so close now, but he could still remember the times when things between them had been rocky, especially when he was younger. Had they too married purely for convenience? Could he and Imogen one day have that too if they married because of the baby—his daughter? Could he forgive and forget the past as Imogen had urged him to just this morning? Could he love his daughter? More importantly, could he give Imogen what she wanted—love?

The thought hung in his mind like icicles in a New York winter. 'You have to be guided by the doctors, Father.' He spoke mechanically, not really part of the conversation, as a turmoil of emotions assailed him. He wasn't fit to be a father. How could he give a child the love it deserved, the love it needed when he'd never known it from his own father?

Imogen came to stand next to him, snapping him from his thoughts, and he pulled up a chair for her next to his father. Wanting to save her from the same kind of inquisitions he'd always endured, the same scolding for not being or doing what was needed, he stood behind her as she sat. He put his hand protectively on her shoulder, trying to let her know that he knew exactly how she must be feeling right now as his father looked from her to him with expectation in his eyes. He wanted her to know he was here for her. After the way he'd reacted at the scan he wanted to make amends, not a need he was familiar with when it came to women, and right now he didn't even know where to begin. All he knew was it mattered to him what she thought, that she wasn't upset any more. It mattered a hell of a lot.

'And I will be, son.' His father looked at Imogen and smiled, but that last word echoed in his mind.

He'd never called him *son* before. As this sank in his father directed the conversation at Imogen. 'And how are you today? I hear the party was a great success, as were you.'

'It was a lovely party. I'm so sorry you had to miss it.' Imogen leaned towards his father and Marco couldn't decide if it was her natural way or she was trying to pull away from him. It was no more than he deserved after the way he'd just treated her.

'Well, I won't miss the next one.' His father laughed, and Marco knew he had to do something to make amends to Imogen, something to redeem himself in her eyes.

'We had a scan today.' Marco dropped the words into the conversation and could almost see the ripples radiating around the room as if he'd just thrown a big stone into a lake. Imogen opened her purse and pulled out the scan image.

'This is our baby.' She handed over the photo and his mother sat on the bed next to his father and looked at it with him, a big, beaming smile on her face. She looked at his father and in that moment Marco knew they loved one another. Whatever had brought them together was still there, despite the rocky road of their marriage. He would never be able to give Imogen that, not after years of fighting for even the smallest show of affection. Every time he'd tried to give his love, every time he'd sought it from his father it had been coldly rejected until he'd locked his heart away, shutting love out of his life. The fear of having his love rejected had been too much. It still was.

'It's a girl,' Marco said firmly, wanting the truth out there, wanting nothing more than to prove to

Imogen he didn't mind if the baby was a boy or a girl. As Imogen looked at him, he saw her eyes glittering. Was that anger or tears? Whatever it was it made him feel like hell. He wasn't going to be able to undo the way he'd acted during the scan with just a few words.

'A girl?' his father asked, and Imogen looked at her hands, now clutched firmly in her lap. He could feel her spirit slipping away, see her confidence and happiness vanishing as her shoulders dropped and her body seemed to weaken with every breath she took. He'd done that to her. If he hadn't said what he'd said at the scan, if he'd let her know, let her feel, that he wanted the baby no matter what, she would be strong enough to take this from his father.

He stood taller as the need to protect Imogen kicked back in. 'Yes, a girl. Not the much coveted Silviano heir.' He heard Imogen's gasp and his sense of inadequacy increased.

'That doesn't matter,' his mother interjected kindly, looking from him to Imogen.

'Of course it matters,' his father growled and Marco wished he'd saved this conversation for a time when Imogen wouldn't have to witness it. 'Any fool can see what you are doing, Marco. You two never planned to marry and if there wasn't a baby you wouldn't even be together.'

Imogen jumped up from the chair and rushed to the door. She turned and looked at him, but he didn't know what to say to make it right for her—hell, he didn't even know what to do. How had his father seen the truth?

Imogen held his gaze for a moment longer then

pulled open the door and fled as if her life depended on it. Marco marched across the room, yanked the door wider and turned to his father. 'What the hell did you do that for?'

'You might not be my biological son, but you are a Silviano.' His father hurled the words at him from the bed. 'Now you need to live up to that name and see what's right in front of you and do the right thing.'

'And what is that?' snapped Marco, torn between the need to finally have this out with his father or go after the only woman who had made him wish he could love and be loved.

'*Dio mio*, Marco. That girl loves you.' Marco froze as his father's voice dropped. He'd never heard such resignation in his voice before. 'It makes no difference what the child is. Don't be the kind of fool I have been. Do the right thing and love her back or damn well let her go!'

Marco's mind raced as his father's admission settled over him. His heart thudded. He looked at his father in silence then turned and ran from the room, sliding round the corner of the corridor and running down it, dodging staff and patients' visitors alike, causing some to berate him. He slid round another corner just in time to see the elevator doors open and Imogen standing there, head bent, looking so lost, so vulnerable that his heart broke.

His heart broke. He stopped as his father's words collided with the realisation of what he felt for Imogen. Was his heart broken because he loved her?

'Imogen, wait,' he called but she didn't hear him. The elevator doors closed, taking her down and away from him.

* * *

Imogen burst out into the sunshine of the afternoon, the sound of New York's streets disorientating her. She'd had to get out of the hospital, away from Marco and the knowledge that he didn't want her or his daughter. As she'd stood in the elevator she'd thought she heard him calling her name, but when the doors closed she'd known it was wishful thinking. Fate had already decreed they didn't belong together.

The cold hardness of his father's voice still rang in her ears. If Marco had grown up with a father like that it wasn't hard to see why he didn't want a family and certainly understandable why he seemed reluctant to allow love into his life. She'd foolishly begun to think that her love might be enough, that staying in New York with him and marrying him would change him simply because she loved him. Now she knew it wasn't going to be anything like that.

How she wished she had Julie to talk to. She glanced at her watch. It was early evening in England. Perfect time to call, but something held her back. She needed to think first, needed to calm her racing heart. She looked around her and saw a wooden seat in the shade of several trees and walked over to it, needing to sit and gather her strength and courage to do what was right.

Marco didn't want a baby girl but needed a son and just now she'd seen exactly why. The man who'd raised him as his own son could only accept a grandson as the next Silviano heir.

She thought of what his mother had said, trying to smooth things over with the assurance that there would be other babies, other chances to have the much-needed male heir. She'd obviously believed her son was engaged, believed they would marry and go on to have more children. But there had been no fooling his father.

She blew out a sigh of frustration, the heat of the afternoon beating down despite summer slipping into the next season. The right thing to do was what was best for her baby, her daughter. After seeing Marco and his father at loggerheads she knew that she had to leave. Today. Now.

Imogen pulled out her phone, dialled Julie and waited while the unfamiliar tone connected her to home. 'Hi, Immy.' Julie's voice crossed the miles and Imogen gulped down her emotions, determined to keep calm. 'The photos on the Empire State Building are so good. I'm really jealous.'

'It's not working,' Imogen butted in before Julie got carried away with something that might have only just happened but now seemed so far in the past it was as if it couldn't have taken place, as if those tender moments in the night before they'd visited the iconic building hadn't happened at all.

'What's not working?' She could hear the confusion in Julie's voice, picture her frowning in that suspicious way she always did.

'Me and Marco.' On the other end of the phone Julie sighed and Imogen closed her eyes then launched into the cold, hard truth of the matter. 'We had a scan today and the baby is a girl, not the boy Marco needs.'

Imogen's hands shook as she held the phone, wishing her friend were here to hug her and make the pain stop. She'd never felt so alone, so isolated from all the people who mattered to her as she did right now.

'What?' Julie's shock raced across the miles and it was as if she were here with her right now, sitting in the afternoon sunshine of New York. It calmed Imogen's panic, but allowed her anger to surface. Anger at Marco. At his father and the ridiculous succession rules his family adhered to.

'You should have heard his voice, Jules, when he knew it was a girl. He sounded as if he was in a business meeting, trying to extract himself from an unsavoury deal. Then his father...' Imogen trailed off as the shock of his father's words stung.

'His father what, Immy?' Julie prodded as silence filled the line.

'His father made it very clear that only a boy was good enough. I couldn't stay there any longer, I just ran.'

'Did Marco come after you?'

'No, it seems pacifying his father is far more important than me or our little girl.' As she said those last two words a sob filled her voice and she took a deep, calming breath, determined not to break down now.

'What do you want to do, Immy?' Julie asked. 'You know I will be here for you no matter what.'

'I don't know,' Imogen confessed. 'I should walk away now, come home and forget him, but I can't.'

Imogen thought of their night together and of the way he'd held her, caressed her, giving her hope that somewhere buried deep beneath the foundations of the barriers he'd built around him was the ability to love. She'd thought she could smash them down, thought she could make a difference to him. She wanted to. 'I love him, Julie.'

'Oh, Immy. Where is Marco now?'

'With his father, I guess.'

Julie sighed again. 'Come home if you want to, Immy, but talk to him first. Tell him how you feel. Just keep me posted on what you are doing.'

'Thanks, Jules,' Imogen whispered as tears threatened once more. She ended the call and sat with her eyes closed as the heat of the sun warmed her face, the background noise of New York calmed her racing mind. Julie was right. She had to talk to Marco. She had to face this head-on, for her sake and her daughter's.

As control slipped back over her she checked her purse. She had a key to Marco's apartment and dollars in her purse. There was nothing stopping her getting into a cab, going back to the apartment and booking a flight home, just as Julie had suggested.

So why wasn't she?

The question raced in her mind.

Because you love him. Because you can't give up on him.

She closed her eyes against the honesty of her answer. She'd fallen in love with Marco. On that last day on the island, as he'd walked with her along the beach to the most amazing night of her life, she'd wished the moment were real, wished they were in love, but past hurt had forced such notions aside. It was why she'd made it easy for Marco to go the next morning. She'd wanted to protect her heart by putting up the barriers. She hadn't wanted the kind of pain she'd experienced after Gavin's betrayal, although she'd never have believed it could feel *this* bad.

Sadness filled her. It wasn't the same for Marco— he hadn't fallen in love with her and never would. For him it had been just sex, both here in New York and on the island. The only difference about the island was that his baby had become a consequence of that sex and now he felt duty bound to her and his father to marry her. That was what his father had said, and Marco had stood there and allowed him to say it. He hadn't tried to protect her or defend her. He hadn't corrected his father at all and as the seconds ticked by whilst she'd stood at the door, ready to flee, she knew he wasn't going to do any of those things.

'Imogen.' Marco's voice sounded behind her, but she refused to turn, refused to acknowledge him.

He stood in front of her and she looked up at him. His dark hair was dishevelled and his tie not straight, as if he'd been dragging it off at some point. He looked more flustered than she'd ever seen him.

'I only have one thing to say to you.' She stood up and looked squarely at him, willing herself to remain calm and composed. She had to tell him it was over, that she was returning to England.

'Don't say it. Not yet,' Marco said, and she frowned at the hint of panic in his voice as he stepped closer, appearing anxious that she might run away again. He knew what she was going to say, he knew, she could see it in his face, in the shadows of his eyes.

'Give me one good reason why I shouldn't.' She stood before him, as tall and straight as she could, finding it bizarre that at a time like this she called upon what she'd learnt in ballet classes as a young child. Not that it mattered one bit, not when she must look a lot more in control and focused than he did right now. She needed to be aloof. Detached.

She'd never seen this side of him, never imagined a

businessman who made millions and oversaw a large global company could look so out of kilter. She could almost feel sorry for him and for a second she nearly did, but with one deep breath she regained the calm indifference she craved.

'My father was aiming all he'd said at me, not you.'

Imogen started to walk away, not wanting to hear his excuses. 'I have no desire to become embroiled in a father-son argument. I want to go back to England. I want my family around me, Marco, family who care—about me and the baby. They won't reject her because she is a girl. They will love her. No matter what.'

'I do care about you and the baby.' He caught hold of her arm, slowing her to a stop when all she wanted to do was rush away and jump in the first taxi she could. Her heart was breaking and the last person she wanted to witness it was Marco. That would give him power over her the way Gavin had had. The power to hurt and humiliate.

'No, Marco.' She rounded on him, vaguely aware of passers-by looking at them. 'You *need* the baby. Remember? That was what you told me in Oxford before I was stupid enough to fly halfway round the world with you. You *need* the baby.' She said it again to drive home her hurt, her indignation. 'But what about me? I guess I'm a part of the deal you have to accept. Or at least that was how it was until you found out the baby is a girl.'

Imogen couldn't help but inject all the frustration and pain which bubbled inside her into her words. Marco's eyes widened in shock and briefly she thought she'd got through to him, made him understand what she felt. Then a glacial hardness settled in his eyes as if the first frost of winter had arrived early.

'You can't even deny it, can you?' She dragged the words out as her heart broke even more at his silence.

Marco looked at Imogen, seeing it from her perspective for the first time. He'd arrived in Oxford and had overheard her conversation with Julie and because of that he'd done the only thing he was comfortable doing and demanded from her what he wanted to happen. Anything else would have meant opening up his emotions, putting himself on the line.

'You've got it all wrong, Imogen,' he said as he reached out to stroke back her hair as the wind whipped it across her face. She backed away from his touch and that stab of panic raced through him again. He was losing her. Losing his baby. All because he'd been hung up on the past. All because he couldn't open his heart to love.

He wanted to blame his father for those harsh words, but knew deep down the old man was right. He'd just been too damn blinded by the desire to gain his father's approval that he hadn't seen what was right before him. He hadn't seen that Imogen loved him.

His father's words played over again in his mind, but the cold and distanced look on Imogen's face made him doubt that. Yet when she'd turned to him this morning as he'd woken to find her looking out over the city, the look on her face had been so very different. Had that been love? Had he thrown it all away?

'Oh, come on, Marco,' she snapped harshly at him.

'You should have heard your shock when you discovered your much-needed son was a girl. A girl you don't need or want.'

'I was a fool.' He took hold of her hand, desperate to keep her from turning away from him, sensing that at any minute she would be gone.

'Yes, you were. I've had enough of fools in my life. First Gavin and now you. It's over, Marco, whatever it is—it's over. I'm going back to England.'

She pulled free of his hand and turned, almost bumping into someone in her haste to get away from him. If his father had been right, if she had loved him, then he had certainly obliterated that love, killed it off as surely as a drought dried up the green grass.

'Imogen, wait.' He rushed after her and for the second time today had to run to try and stop her leaving. 'Imogen,' he called again more sharply.

She didn't turn, didn't even pause, but reached the pavement and all but walked out in front of a taxi in a bid to get it to stop. He increased his pace and managed to grab the open taxi door as she climbed in. He threw himself into the taxi after her as he heard her give his address.

'Silviano's Coffee House,' he said to the driver, cancelling out her request. He wasn't ready to let her go yet, although he didn't know if he could do what his father had told him—love her or let her go. Either was an extreme he couldn't contemplate.

'What do you think you are doing?' she gasped as she moved as far across the taxi as she could. He was sure if it hadn't moved off into the flow of traffic she would have bailed out the other side.

'I got it wrong, very wrong, and if you must go I understand, but before you do I want to show you something.'

'Why should I listen to anything you have to say, much less believe it?' Her eyes spat fiery indignation at him.

'Because it's part of your child's heritage. It's part of who your daughter will be.'

CHAPTER ELEVEN

IMOGEN GLARED AT Marco across the taxi. Damn him. Even now he was playing with her emotions, toying with the family values she held so dear. All she wanted was to get away, from him, his family and New York. It wouldn't take her long to pack her few belongings and book a flight. She could be on her way home tonight. But if she indulged him in this she would miss the last flight back and have to stay with him at his apartment—unless she booked into a hotel instead.

'Part of who my daughter will be?' she challenged, not prepared to back down now she'd made her mind up to leave. 'How can you say that? You are using the one thing that means so much to me just to get what *you* want. And the only thing I can assume is that it's so you appear not to be turning your back on me or your child. After all, it's a girl—and girls don't count, do they?'

'Yes, I am trying to get what I want, Imogen,' he said slowly and sat back calmly in the taxi as if the fact that she was talking to him meant he'd already won. It just made her more convinced that walking away now was the right thing to do—for all of them.

'I'm leaving, Marco. Tonight. We both want very different things from this arrangement. As soon as we learnt the baby is a girl everything went wrong. It's for the best, for all of us, and you know it.'

'Very well, if you feel that's what you must do.' Marco's words shocked Imogen into a brief silence and she looked at him, trying to second-guess what he was really planning. 'But at least give me the chance to show you something. All I ask for is an hour.'

'One hour, Marco.' She kept her voice firm, despite the temptation to believe he might have changed. That would never happen. 'You've got one hour. Then I'm going back to the apartment to pack my things and book a flight.'

'One hour,' he agreed, his voice softer, more like that of the Marco she'd first met on the island. She watched him as he focused on the road ahead, as if not trusting the taxi driver to take them to his destination instead of hers. Something inside her melted a little as he inhaled deeply, giving her a sense that the emotional barriers he'd built around himself were gradually slipping away as they drove through the city.

She couldn't look at him any more. He would strip away all the anger, all the fight and conviction that she was doing the right thing. He would suffocate all that detachment and aloofness she'd fought hard to carry off. Part of her wanted to force him to look at her, force him to hear the truth of why she couldn't stay, but sense prevailed. He didn't want love in his life and certainly wouldn't want to hear her say 'I love you'. She was also certain he wouldn't understand that she had to leave *because* she loved him.

'We are almost there.' He turned to face her, and his gaze locked with hers. She held her breath as that all-too-familiar attraction crackled in the air around them. Whenever he looked at her like that it was as if they had been transported back to the island. But the island was escapism. This was reality.

'Where?' To her horror the word had become a husky whisper, showing her vulnerability to him all over again. She tried again, forcing harshness into the word. 'Where?'

'Our baby is the next Silviano heir. My heir and I don't care if it's a boy or a girl.'

She opened her mouth to protest, to remind him how disgusted he was with the prospect of a daughter, but he pressed his finger to her lips, the gesture so intimate it shocked her into silence. He pulled his finger away, looking as shocked as she was that he'd done it, and she couldn't help but wet her lips with her tongue, tasting him, feeling the heat his touch had left behind. The wild thumping of her heart and the heat curling deep inside from that simple action proved she was far from indifferent to him, something she really didn't want Marco to know.

'I want to show you where it all began.' Marco's voice held determination as the taxi pulled up. Saddened that this would be the final time they were together, she watched him as he took out his wallet, handing over the dollars for the fare.

She'd never forget how his dark hair curled at the back of his neck, especially when it was wet from the sea. Or the feel of his stubble when he'd kissed her in the morning. More than that, for ever etched in her memory would be the way he'd caressed her body, the heat of his kiss, the sensation as he'd made her completely his and the amazing heights he'd taken her to. Whatever happened, whatever he said or did next, she didn't think she'd ever forget that.

Imogen dragged herself from memories that wouldn't help her now as Marco opened the door and got out, the sounds of the streets rushing in at her. She was tired, upset. She wasn't in the mood for mysteries, but if what he'd said was true and this was about his family's past, their child's family, then she owed it to her little girl, and Marco, to give him this time.

Weariness seeped into her as the seesaw of emotions of the last few hours began to take its toll. She slipped along the seat of the taxi and got out, taking Marco's hand as he offered it to her. Instantly she wished she hadn't as the heat of his touch raced up her arm and charged round her body, reminding her of just how she'd spent last night and the early hours of this morning.

How had everything turned so wrong? This morning she'd been happy, so very happy, and had even begun to believe there was a future for them, then in a matter of minutes all that had changed, getting worse with each passing hour.

'This is what I want to show you,' Marco said as they stood on the pavement outside an Italian coffee shop that looked as if it had been there for decades.

'This?' she queried and looked up at the tall, narrow brick building before looking again at the sign above the wooden windows: *Silviano's Coffee Shop*.

Marco watched Imogen as she looked at the building and then read the sign above the window. The late-afternoon sun was shining in her hair, reminding him of that last day on the beach as they'd walked back to the villa after the snorkelling trip. The sun had high-lighted her beauty to perfection that afternoon and it was doing the same now. He'd treasure that image for the rest of his life.

The thought that he might lose her rushed at him like a spring tide. He couldn't lose her now. He just couldn't. But if he didn't get this right, didn't show her all his family had done and why it was so impor-tant to carry on the family name, then that was ex-actly what he might do. The prospect pushed him on.

'Silviano's,' he said proudly. 'Started by my grand-parents after they'd immigrated to New York from Sicily.'

Imogen gasped softly, looked from him to the cof-fee shop and back to him again. 'This is the actual shop? It's still part of the company?'

'Yes, and very much part of my life. Shall we?' He gestured towards the door, knowing that if he could get her inside he had a fighting chance of proving who he really was and more importantly telling her why he didn't want her to leave. But confessing to an emotion he'd locked out of his life for so long was not an easy thing to contemplate. He didn't even know if he could say those words she needed to hear because if he ever said them he had to mean it, had to have been able to put his past behind him. He just wasn't sure yet if he was ready for either of those scenarios.

'Okay,' she said softly, and he hoped he was begin-ning to break past the defensive wall that had rushed up after that scene in the hospital with his father. 'Just for a while.'

He opened the brown wooden door and stepped in, the aroma of coffee greeting him. Italian music drifted subtly in the background. The lady behind the counter, which was laden with pastries and delicacies, greeted him in Italian as she did each week when he called in. His visits allowed him to feel close to his grandfather, the only person other than his mother who had given him unconditional love as a child. The man he'd always thought of as his father had never seemed capable of love, but here, with his grandfather, that had always existed. It was why he'd fought to keep the place open. Because it had meant something to his grandfather and that was important.

'What would you like to drink? Espresso?' He pulled out a chair and waited as Imogen sat down. She looked up at him as he stood behind her and in his mind it was last night again. They had been standing in front of his windows as he'd slowly undressed her, revealing her sexy body, which never failed to rouse his ardour. He could still taste her skin on his lips as if he'd only just trailed kisses down her shoulders.

'I'll just have an Americano, with milk.' She turned from him and looked around at the array of photos on the wall, as if looking into his eyes was too much for her. Again, he played his father's words in his mind, again wondering if she did love him and, if so, how could his father see it and be so sure when he himself hadn't had a clue?

Marco placed the order then sat at his regular table. 'That's my grandfather and grandmother there.' He pointed to the black and white image of his grandparents standing outside the coffee shop which hung on the wall above the table. 'And that is my parents on their wedding day.'

'Did they run this place too?' she asked as their coffees arrived.

'No, my father didn't want to continue what my grandfather had started and opened hotels in New York instead. I took it one step further and made the Silviano company a global concern, but unlike my father, who'd allowed this place to almost close, I wanted to keep it open, keep it going. It's part of my family history and now part of our daughter's.'

She smiled at him and lightness filled him. This was what he'd hoped for, that showing her he was a man who honoured and respected family might mean she would at least stay a while longer. Give him more of a chance to prove they did have something worth saving and that he did want to be a father to his child—boy or girl.

'What about your father, your natural father?' Imogen asked the question tentatively.

'That's him up there.' He pointed at a much smaller black and white photo and tried to quell his annoyance at what his mother had kept from him all these years. Why, he still didn't know, but over the last few days the importance he'd put on that had begun to fade. He drew his focus back on what he needed to do, needed to say. 'I wish I'd known who he really was.'

'Your mother must have had good reasons not to tell you.' Imogen's words only reinforced what he'd just thought and once again he knew with certainty that it didn't matter any more. 'And it certainly seems they are in love now.'

Love. There was that word again.

Questions raced in his mind as he asked himself again if he loved her, if he was able to give her what she wanted. He still couldn't answer that, but he knew that if he stood any chance of keeping Imogen here, keeping her in his life then love was something he would have to talk about, although he was far from ready to admit he loved anyone. He'd long ago learnt that opening himself up to such emotions only hurt. Locking his feelings away, making himself hard to reach had become a natural defensive action. One he wasn't sure he would ever be able to stop doing.

'I had never had my father marked out as a man who loved,' Marco began as he tried to divert the conversation away from himself, away from the two of them, at least until she knew all he had to tell her. He swigged back his espresso in one go, signalling for another. 'My father certainly never allowed me to feel loved.'

Imogen touched his hand and he looked at her, the honesty in her eyes almost too much. 'He must have loved you, Marco. He brought you up as his son.'

'Only because he didn't have a son of his own. I could never live up to his expectations and I don't believe I will ever be able to do so.'

'Why do you shut people out, Marco? Why do you deny yourself love?'

He looked at her, seeing the softness in her eyes as she held her head at an angle, looking as innocently beguiling as she did sexy. 'I'm not the only one shutting myself away, am I, Imogen? Isn't that what you were doing when we were on the island? Locking your heart away?'

Ever since she'd spoken of Gavin when they'd been

on the top of the Empire State Building, he'd known that was why she'd walked away from him, away from the magical week they had enjoyed so easily on the island, and probably why she'd been so reluctant to find him and tell him about the pregnancy. He could still hear that reluctance now if he replayed Imogen's conversation he'd overheard with Julie the day his life had changed for ever.

'Gavin hurt me. He threw my love back at me like some discarded object, preferring to seek it elsewhere. Hurt like that is hard to forget.' The passion in her voice left him in no doubt she'd loved her ex-fiancé and jealousy raged through him.

'Whereas my hurt, my inability to love or be loved is much more long standing?' He couldn't keep the sharpness from his voice and once again threw back his espresso in one gulp, needing the caffeine hit it was giving him. Why the hell couldn't he just tell her how he felt about her?

'I didn't mean that,' she said, and looked into her cup as if it held the answers to all their problems. 'Didn't you ever feel love, Marco? What about when you were a boy?'

'When I was younger I spent most of my time here, with my grandparents. Knowing what I do now, I guess that's because they wanted to give me what was missing, what my father didn't or couldn't give me.'

As he said that he realised there had been love in his life, he'd just been so consumed by the desire to please his father, gain his approval, he'd shut himself away a bit more each time he'd failed, locking out the good as well as the bad. Then when first his grandmother and then his grandfather had passed away the light of love had gone out in his life, and he'd become detached from his family, unreachable.

'How old were you then?' She tentatively asked the question, her eyes searching his as if looking for the answer to this and so much more.

'Twelve years old.' He pressed his jaw tight as he remembered the day he'd realised the two people that meant the most to him, the two people who'd loved him unconditionally, had gone from his life.

'And now you don't think anyone can love you?' That question spun around his mind and he looked at Imogen. Was his father right? Did she love him?

'And you don't trust yourself to love anyone?' Her voice was firmer as she spoke again, negating the need for him to answer. She was forcing him to understand, forcing him to accept his past.

He rubbed his hand over his jaw, feeling the new growth of stubble, and looked at Imogen. She'd got it so right that it made any kind of response impossible for a moment. She was right. He didn't trust himself to love and he'd already hurt Imogen really badly. He didn't deserve her love. Once again, his father's words played in his mind.

Love her or let her go.

He couldn't love her, but he cared for her. He cared enough to not want to hurt her any more than he had done already. He cared enough to let her go.

He nodded. 'I did tell you on the island that love would never be part of my life and I know that's what you want. But I can't give it to you, Imogen. I can care for you and the baby, give you both every material thing you could want, but I can't promise I can ever allow love back into my life.'

* * *

Ice rushed through Imogen, despite the heat of the summer and the coffee. She was frozen to the core. Every last bit of love she'd been trying to suppress had turned solid. Marco didn't want her love, didn't want to love her. He didn't even want to try. He was as good as telling her to walk away now.

She stood up and pushed back her chair. 'Thank you for showing me the photos, for allowing me to see some of our daughter's family history.'

Marco glanced at his watch then up at her. Had he been marking time whilst he'd told her all she needed to know? At first she'd hoped he was going to tell her that he hadn't had love in his life, that until he'd met her he hadn't fallen in love. She stupidly thought he was going to tell her she'd changed that. How silly was she to believe that she could change anything, change him?

'You said family was important to you.' He stood up as if he was already ringing time on their conversation. He wasn't going to tell her anything else and he certainly wasn't going to try and dissuade her from leaving.

'It is. And I'm going back to my family, Marco. Back to the people who love me.'

His brows flicked up briefly then he pushed in his chair. It was over. He was letting her walk away and Imogen's heart broke completely. Marco didn't want her, didn't love her. 'I will, of course, always support you and the baby.'

The baby he didn't want. The daughter he didn't need. If she kept that in the forefront of her mind instead of focusing on the love he didn't want from her, the love he couldn't give her in return, then she would remain determined and strong. She'd be driven by anger instead of regret and that was going to be the only way to get through this.

'In that case—' she stood tall as she spoke and looked him in the eyes, fuelled now by the sudden strength which had rushed through her '—there is nothing left to say, Marco—except goodbye.'

CHAPTER TWELVE

SLEEP HAD BEEN fitful for Marco the night after Imogen had left. He'd returned later that evening to his apartment to find her few belongings gone. He was sure he'd done the right thing for Imogen by letting her go. It was his father's words which had convinced him, but the little sleep he had had that night had been steeped in dreams of Imogen. Dreams of her laughing on the island when they'd been so carefree. Her face full of desire as she'd turned to face him that night in his apartment, before allowing the gold silk of her dress to cascade down her, enabling him to see his child in her tummy for the first time.

As dawn had broken over the city he'd known for sure he'd done the wrong thing. He should never have let the woman he loved walk out of his life. His father's words might have sounded harsh, but Marco had finally accepted he'd been trying to tell him to let go of the past, to look to the future—with Imogen—and, most important of all, to allow himself to love her.

As his overnight flight had touched down in Heathrow this morning he'd even wanted to ring his father and thank him for opening his eyes and his heart to something so precious. But there hadn't been time for that. He had to see her as soon as he could. Imogen would almost certainly have flown home the same night as she'd walked out of the café. All he'd focused on was hiring a car and getting to Oxford. Getting to Imogen.

Now as he rang the bell on the modest house set in a small village outside Oxford his heart was thudding. What if she wouldn't see him? What if he was too late to tell her he loved her?

The aged wooden door opened. 'May I see Imogen, please?' This must be her father. There was a family resemblance that was very strong and it made him ever more desperate to see her, to put things right, once and for all.

'You must be Marco.' Suspicion filled every word.

'I am. I really need to see her,' he said as the man stood like a sentry on the threshold, preventing him from seeing the woman he loved. 'I should never have let her walk away. *Dio mio*, I was a fool.'

'At least you can admit that much,' her father said, still standing his ground.

'Can I see her?' Did the man want him to beg? He wasn't used to having to cajole people round to his way of thinking. Here he was on the brink of admitting to love, the one thing he'd shut out of his life, and he had to get past an over-protective father.

What would he do if it was his daughter, his little girl? Would he stand back and let the man who'd almost certainly broken her heart back into her life? Would he like hell! A furious rush of protective emotions surged over him. He'd never let anyone hurt his little girl. Least of all a man like him—or the blind and stubborn man he'd been.

Again, that wave of doubt rushed over him. The thought that he didn't deserve love, couldn't give love, tried to forge forwards. But not this time. This time he wasn't going to allow it. This time, once and for all, he was going to stamp it out. He didn't want to be the same man his father was and more importantly he wanted Imogen to know that. He had to tell her he loved her, even if it was too late; he had to tell her.

'Mr Fraser, I appreciate I've upset Imogen—'

'That's an understatement.' Her father cut across his words and he knew he deserved every bit of contempt that was in the other man's voice.

He ran his fingers through his hair, becoming exasperated with the conversation, and turned away to look at his hired car parked in the country lane. As he turned back, the door opened wider and a small woman looked at him. There was no doubt this was Imogen's mother.

'Can I please see Imogen?'

'She's not here yet,' her mother volunteered in the same soft voice Imogen had, making his heart constrict just to hear it.

'Yet? What do you mean?'

'She's flying home tonight. She will be on the last flight in from New York to Heathrow this evening.'

Relief surged through Marco. 'I will meet the flight,' he said, adding quickly when he saw the warning frown on her father's face, 'And bring her home.' With barely a word of thanks he rushed back to the car. This evening couldn't come soon enough.

One night in an economy hotel in New York and over eight hours in the confines of Standard Class, on the first flight she'd been able to get back to Heathrow, had left Imogen bone-weary, tired and emotionally numb. All she wanted was to sleep in her childhood room, with her favourite teddies still on the bed. She smiled weakly at the thought as she grabbed her case and made her way with the throng of passengers through to Arrivals.

Squeals of delight caught her attention as one man dropped his case and ran into the arms of a woman, swinging her round and kissing her. That was true love and one day she hoped she would find it. Moving around him, still smiling, she continued past the many people waiting with signs. Then she saw him.

Marco.

Standing right in front of her.

He'd discarded his suit for jeans and a shirt. He looked amazing and her heart thudded, her breath wouldn't come easily, and she slowed to a stop, letting go of her case. She stood there, her gaze locked with his, not daring to walk towards him, not daring to believe he was really there. The distance between them seemed too great, too insurmountable and far too dangerous for her broken heart.

Other passengers jostled her as they made their way past, either desperate to get to their destination or meet family and friends. Imogen just stood, aware she was in the way, aware she must look as if she'd lost her mind, but she couldn't move.

Marco was here.

He'd arrived in England before her? Did that mean he wanted her? She dared to hope and as if in slow motion she watched him walk towards her. Her heart thumped as he came closer, enabling her to see his eyes more clearly, see the emotion in them. His expression was his usual cool-and-in-control businessman, but in his eyes she could see trepidation. Doubt. Even fear. And something else.

Her heart lurched as hope flooded through her, washing away the tiredness as he moved towards her before stopping again.

'Imogen,' he finally said and stopped a few paces away from her. Was that to force her to come to him or fear of what she might say? She couldn't move towards him and, even though he was so close, that distance seemed impossible.

'What are you doing here, Marco?' Her voice was so quiet, barely above a whisper, and she glanced away from Marco, noticing that the people immediately around them had stopped what they were doing, that they were watching this exchange between her and Marco.

'You left something behind,' he said as he moved a few steps closer. He wasn't close enough to touch, but if she closed her eyes she was sure she'd be able to feel him near.

She thought of the engagement ring she'd replaced in its box before leaving, placing it on the glass table in the middle of his living area. She'd stood there and looked at it, knowing that, as beautiful as it was, it didn't stand for what she wanted. It meant possession for Marco. Possession of a son, not the declaration of love she wanted it to represent. It meant nothing to her and her daughter.

'I didn't leave anything, Marco,' she said, her breath catching as he took the final steps towards her and put out his hand, opening it to reveal the engagement ring.

The gathering crowd gasped as he stood there, hand outstretched, with the large gemstone sparkling beneath the bright lights of the airport.

'You left this.'

Emotions threatened to overwhelm her. He was here. All this way and he was here to meet her off the plane, but she didn't want the ring. She just wanted to hear him say those three precious words. The same words she wanted to say to him, but fear of his rejection kept them locked inside.

She shook her head, refusing to reach out for the ring, refusing to do anything other than look at it. She couldn't even look into the face of the man she loved.

'You also left me,' he said softly.

She finally looked up and a sparkle of humour had slipped into his eyes, playing havoc with her emotions. If only he'd say it. If only he'd forget the past and allow love into his life. If he said it, told her he loved her, even once, she'd be his for evermore.

Marco wanted to shout it out that he loved this woman, but still his past clung to him. He could see the confusion mixed with hope in her eyes. If he didn't say it now, if he didn't finally put the past behind him, he would lose Imogen for ever. It didn't matter that they were in the middle of the airport, or that a crowd was watching with interest, some even filming it on their phones—he had to tell her. He had to tell her now. No matter who was watching, no matter who was listening to his every word.

'Imogen.' He took her left hand, buoyed by the fact that she didn't pull away, that she didn't resist. Her eyes filled with tears as he placed the ring back on her finger. He swallowed, took a deep breath. 'Imogen Fraser, I love you and I want to marry you.'

The crowd became hushed with expectation as she looked at him, her eyes so blue and filled with emotion. Her silence nearly killed him. He willed her to say something, willed her to accept his love.

There was nothing for it. Marco threw caution to the wind and smashed down the final remnants of the barriers he'd built round his heart and got down on one knee. He looked up at Imogen, still holding her hand, as the gathered crowd oohed and aahed.

'Imogen Fraser, will you make me the happiest man in the world and marry me?'

'I don't know what to say,' she whispered.

'Say yes,' one of the people in the crowd shouted, but his eyes never left hers and the tension was almost too much.

'I'm sorry. For everything, and if you don't say yes I don't know what I am going to do because I'm madly in love with you, Imogen.'

'What about the baby?' He saw her swallow after the words and knew this was as hard for her as it was for him.

'I already love my little girl—because she is part of you.'

'But she isn't the son you want, the son you need.' Her voice was strained with tears as her eyes begged him, pleaded with him to understand.

'That doesn't matter to me, Imogen. You told me this is the twenty-first century and I will change that—our daughter will have as much right to inherit as any other child we have.'

A lady in the gathered crowd cooed over his declaration, but nothing could stop him from declaring his love for Imogen now. He didn't care how many people witnessed it.

'Are you sure?' she asked, her face full of disbelief.

'I've never been more certain of anything in my life, Imogen. When you left it was as if someone had turned the lights of New York out; even though every building glowed and sparkled, the whole city was dark to me. You brought light and love into my life, Imogen, and if you don't want me then my world will be dark for evermore.'

She drew in a deep, shuddering breath and he held his, waiting for what she'd say. Instead she pulled her hands free of his and he waited, still on one knee. Time hung tensely around them and the sounds of the busy airport filtered in.

She reached out, took his hand and pulled gently. He stood up and looked down at her, waiting, hoping. Then she smiled and flung her arms around his neck, hugging him tight against her.

The crowd cheered, and he closed his eyes in relief, holding her tighter than he'd ever held her before, but when she pulled back he was forced to slacken his hold. He looked into her eyes, saw the happiness there, but more than that he saw what he'd missed all along: her love.

'Don't ever leave me again, Imogen.' His husky words were silenced by her kiss and he gave himself up to it, feeling the rising heat of desire. The crowd clapped and cheered harder and Imogen pulled away, suddenly shy and coy as she looked around at them, then back to him.

She looked up at him from lowered lashes, a soft flush on her cheeks. 'I love you, Marco Silviano, and the answer is yes.'

'Answer?' he teased, elation taking over the tension which had kept him rooted to the spot as she'd walked through Arrivals.

'To your question?' She was laughing at him now, as were the still gathered crowd of people.

'Oh, that question,' he said as he laughed with her. 'Then I had better ask it again, whilst we have all these witnesses to your answer. Imogen Fraser, will you do me the honour of becoming my wife?'

'Absolutely I will.' She laughed softly.

He silenced her laughter with a kiss, one so demanding, so full of passion *and* love that someone told him to get a room. Imogen laughed against his lips and he reluctantly pulled back to look at her.

'Should we?' she asked provocatively. 'Get a room?'

He put on an expression of shock. 'Not when I promised your father I would bring you home.'

'I don't care where I go, just as long as you come too.' She snuggled against him and he held her close, watching as the crowd drifted away, losing interest now he'd been put out of his misery.

He kissed the top of her head, smelt the unique scent of the woman he loved and sent a silent message to his father for pushing him to do this with his somewhat harsh comment and he knew he'd finally done the right thing, finally earned his approval.

EPILOGUE

MARCO WAS WAITING for Imogen on the beach, dressed in a tuxedo and holding champagne and glasses. He smiled and as usual her heart filled with happiness. They'd been married for one year and had a beautiful daughter, Sofia, whom Marco idolised. Now he'd whisked her away to his island retreat, telling her he wanted her all to himself on their first anniversary.

Imogen kissed him lightly on the lips as she took her champagne from him, anticipation warming her as she thought of spending another night alone on the beach with Marco.

'Happy anniversary,' he said and chinked his glass against hers, his eyes dark with desire.

'Happy anniversary,' she said softly, smiling up at him. 'I hope you haven't got a crowd ready assembled again. I couldn't bear to have any more videos of us going viral.'

She couldn't help but tease, as she often did about his declaration of love at the airport. He always claimed he paid all those people to gather round, and cheer him on, but she knew better than that. The video someone had posted had soon been everywhere, even in Marco's business fields. Not that she minded one bit.

'Not a crowd exactly.' Mischief lingered in his voice and she looked suspiciously at him.

'What have you done this time, Marco?' She knew instantly he was up to something and she challenged him with mock disapproval.

'I might have invited a few friends and family members out here to help us celebrate.'

'A few?' she questioned, teasing him ever more.

'A bit more than a few,' he confessed. 'There is nobody else on the island but our family and friends and they are waiting for us where we first met.'

'All of them?' Imogen thought of the little girl she'd reluctantly left in the care of her mother. It was the first time she'd left her for more than just a night and it had pulled at her heartstrings, even though she really wanted some quality time alone with Marco.

'All of them, including little Sofia.'

'I love you, Marco,' she said as she kissed him gently on the lips and then smiled up at him. 'That's such a romantic and thoughtful gesture.' She kissed him once more, almost spilling her champagne as passion took over and she forgot herself.

Marco held Imogen's hand as they arrived at the restaurant where he'd arranged for everyone to be as part of the surprise, but when Imogen saw Sofia in her grandmother's arms she let his hand go and rushed to her daughter. He knew being apart from their daughter for any length of time was hard for her.

'She's certainly got her mother's sweet nature.' His father came to stand by him, passing him a glass of champagne. 'I just hope when you have a little boy he won't be as stubborn or difficult as you once were.'

Marco laughed, knowing full well his father was teasing him, and happy he'd made a full recovery from the complications after his heart surgery. 'All Silviano males are stubborn, Father, regardless of age.'

'True.' His father nodded over to where Imogen was laughing with Julie and her new fiancé. They were all making a fuss of Sofia in her gorgeous little party dress. 'Your wife is a wonderful woman, Marco.'

He and his father had got on much better since he'd come to his senses and opened his heart to Imogen and love, but he'd never yet had the chance to ask the reason for the secrecy behind who his natural father was. He'd never had that opening, one that wouldn't catapult them back to troubled waters.

'Is that what you thought of Mother when you asked her to marry you?'

His father looked at him, then his gaze drifted around their guests, finally settling on his wife. 'I have loved your mother since the day we first met, and I still loved her after the affair, even though the child she carried may not have been mine. I still loved her, still wanted to marry her. Our marriage may have been a difficult one in those early days, but my love for her has always been stronger than my pride.'

Marco emptied his glass and put it down, turning to his father, finally able to put to rest the last bit of his past.

'What about me?'

'You?' His father smiled. 'You were a bonus, a very trying one at times, but a bonus none the less. You were the son I always wanted. I just didn't realise that as I pushed you harder to succeed it was driving us further apart. It was all done out of love for you, my son.'

Imogen joined them at that moment and little Sofia reached for her much adored *nonno*. Marco watched as he took the little girl in his arms, saw the smile and the love and knew that nothing from the past mattered any more. He had the love of the woman he was hopelessly in love with and a beautiful daughter. He'd mended bridges with his family. He couldn't want for more.

He took Imogen's hand and led her away, pausing briefly to talk to her parents, who were totally smitten by the island. As soon as they were alone he kissed her. A deep and lingering kiss, one filled with the love that was in his heart.

'Happy?' he asked her as she snuggled against him.

'Yes. Having friends and family here is such a lovely surprise, thank you. Although...' Her voice trailed off and he tilted her chin up, forcing her to look into his eyes. The temptation to kiss her was great, but he also wanted to hear why she wasn't completely thrilled about their guests.

'Although what?'

'I had been kind of hoping we could have a night alone on the beach again. See if we can create a little brother for Sofia.'

Marco raised his brows. 'You are very bad, Imogen Silviano, tempting a man away from his guests like that.'

Imogen smiled coyly at him. 'Just one night. You, me, the moon and the stars and the sound of the ocean.'

He pulled her into his arms, his heart swelling with love for her. 'How can I resist such an offer?' He kissed her lips, grazing his over hers, teasing the desire from her. 'I love you, Imogen. So very much.'

* * * * *

COMING SOON!

We really hope you enjoyed reading this book. If you're looking for more romance, be sure to head to the shops when new books are available on

Thursday 15th November

MILLS & BOON

Coming next month

MARRIED FOR HIS ONE-NIGHT HEIR
Jennifer Hayward

'What were you going to tell Leo when the time came? The truth? Or were you going to tell him that his father was a high-priced thug?'

She flinched. Lifted a fluttering hand to her throat. 'I hadn't thought that far ahead,' she admitted. 'We've been too busy trying to survive. Making a life for ourselves. Leo's welfare has been my top priority.'

Which he believed. It was the only reason he wasn't going to take his child and walk. Do to her exactly what she'd done to him. Because as angry as he was, as unforgivable as what she had done had been, he had to take the situation she'd been in into account. It had taken guts for her to walk away from her life. Courage. She'd put Leo first, something his own mother hadn't done. And she had been young and scared. All things he couldn't ignore.

Gia set her gaze on his, apprehension flaring in her eyes. 'I can't change the past, Santo, the decisions I made. But I can make this right. Clearly,' she acknowledged, 'you are going to want to be a part of Leo's life. I was thinking about solutions last night. I thought you could visit us here... Get Leo used to the idea of having you around, and then, when he is older, more able to understand the situation, we can tell him the truth.'

A slow curl of heat unraveled inside of him, firing the blood in his veins to dangerously combustible levels. 'And what do you propose we tell him when I visit? That I am that *friend* you referred to the other night? How many *friends* do you have, Gia?'

Her face froze. 'I have been building a *life* here. Establishing a career. There has been no time for dating. All I do is work and spend time with Leo, who is a handful as you can imagine, as all three-year-olds tend to be.'

The defensively issued words lodged themselves in his throat. 'I can't actually imagine,' he said softly, 'because you've deprived me of the right to know that, Gia. You have deprived me of *everything*.'

She blanched. He set down his glass on the bar. 'I am his *father*. I have missed three years of his life. You think a *weekend pass* is going to suffice? A few dips in the sea as he learns to swim?' He shook his head. 'I want *every day* with him. I want to wake up with him bouncing on the bed. I want to take him to the park and throw a ball around. I want to hear about his day when I tuck him into bed. I want it *all*.'

'What else can we do?' she queried helplessly. 'You live in New York and I live here. Leo is settled and happy. A limited custody arrangement is the only realistic solution for us.'

'It is *not* a viable proposition.' His low growl made her jump. 'That's not how this is going to work, Gia.'

She eyed him warily. 'Which part?'

'All of it. I have a proposal for you. It's the only one on the table. Nonnegotiable on all points. Take it or leave it.'

The wariness written across her face intensified. 'Which is?'

'We do what's in the best interests of our child. You marry me, we create a life together in New York and give Leo the family he deserves.'

Continue reading
MARRIED FOR HIS ONE-NIGHT HEIR
Jennifer Hayward

www.millsandboon.co.uk

LET'S TALK
Romance

For exclusive extracts, competitions
and special offers, find us online:

- facebook.com/millsandboon
- @MillsandBoon
- @MillsandBoonUK

Get in touch on 01413 063232

For all the latest titles coming soon, visit
millsandboon.co.uk/nextmonth